I SPY, YOU DIE

I SPY, YOU DIE

A NOVEL

by

HOSANNA BROWN

LONDON
VICTOR GOLLANCZ LTD
1984

None of the characters in this novel bear any intended similarity to any real people. Michaelhouse College, Cambridge, was founded in 1324 but it no longer exists today. The University of Cambridge and its laboratories have no relation to what is portrayed in this novel. Only Heffer's bookstore is real.

The words of the song quoted on page 166, *Ice Cream, You Scream* by Howard Johnson–Robert King–Billy Moll, are copyright and are reprinted by permission of Shapiro-Bernstein Company Inc., New York.

British Library Cataloguing in Publication Data
Brown, Hosanna
I spy, you die.
I. Title
823[F]   PR9619.3.B/

ISBN 0-575-03435-1

Photoset in Great Britain by
Rowland Phototypesetting Limited, Bury St Edmunds, Suffolk
and printed by St Edmundsbury Press
Bury St Edmunds, Suffolk

I

'WELL, WHAT WOULD you expect of a self-avowed virgin?' Dr Patrick Most, Master of Michaelhouse, extended an angular forefinger and thumb to pick at the hollow stem of his Moselle glass before finally raising it, in front of the light as if to examine the curlicues etched across crystal. And then to his lips. No delicate sip, a hearty swig, the glass almost emptied. To be at once refilled by an expectant waiter, suaver than any guest.

This remark was tossed, languidly, like a salad, at Mr James Thorpe. Looking uncomfortable in his brocaded white shirt and starched collar, sweating already. Smoked salmon piled upon his plate—was there even more than on everyone else's?

Frank le Roux, dining for the first time at High Table of a college in the illustrious University of Cambridge—of the second oldest college at that, as the Master had informed her over sherry. He always did. It wasn't the second best so why not boast about what one could. Frank caught the Master's current remark over the northern drawl of her neighbour on the other side, Dr Simon Jeffrey. A sort of lecture about Dr Samuel Johnson and what a nice man he really was. There seemed to be a lot of mini-lectures going on around the table. The way academics often communicated, Frank reflected. As if they had a panel of little buttons on their stomachs, you pressed one, and it spouted forth on a favourite topic.

Except that the most interesting oration seemed to be directed at rich Mr Thorpe. That was why he was there, Frank had been told in a very loud whisper. Not that he knew anything, or anyone, but the fellow had money, don't you know. 'Money', the word had been spat out like a lump of stale phlegm. Unpleasant, not really the sort of thing one wanted to mention at dinner, let alone at an official Feast. But necessary. For refronting the hall, renovating the bell-tower. And even for providing a new wing of rooms for all those beastly undergraduates one was forced to teach nowadays, Simon Jeffrey had concluded.

Last month, the story went, a scruffy old man had bumbled into the bursar's office and said he was interested in contributing to the building appeal. Could he see the plans please, and also the exact site where it was to be erected. The bursar had disdainfully waved his most junior assistant into action. Mr Thorpe pored over the plans for a good half-hour and then poked with his stick at the lawn over against Trinity. Finally he announced that the site was quite suitable. He'd have to consult his lawyer about the exact sum but it would be of the order of two million, give or take a couple of hundred thousand.

Thus was this elderly recluse, potentate of the car-rental market, invited to share the Feast of the Apparition of St Michael with the cream (self-considered) of English intelligentsia. James Thorpe, who as a boy had gazed across the street at begowned undergraduates like something from another planet (or from a zoo?). James Thorpe, who had worked from the age of twelve, leaving himself no time for leisure or wives or hobbies. Who had never read a book in his life. James Thorpe now turned to the scarlet-robed figure on his other side, Sir Barry Stone, Director of the Kavendish Laboratory, for some explanation of the Master's cryptic snub.

Frank strained across Simon's incantation about Boswell and the Hebrides to catch Sir Barry's comment. *Who* was a self-avowed virgin, for goodness sake? It was just possible to decipher Stone's antipodean diphthongs in between keeping up a show of interest by 'uh-hu', 'I see' and 'what happened next?' to the Johnsonian monologue.

'He's right, you know, Mr Thorpe. Made a few discoveries about gravitation in his youth but all Isaac was really interested in was alchemy, turning lead into gold.' Mr Thorpe's eyes lit up, as if that might be rather a good idea.

'And Newton spent most of his life on religion. Funny sort of stuff he wrote. Did you know he was an anti-Trinitarian? Pretty good for a Trinity man, what!' The Master smote his thigh with one hand while simultaneously re-emptying the glass with the other, waiting for it to be refilled, and then downing half of that. (Why didn't he use a bigger one in the first place, Frank wondered. After all, he's the boss.)

Simon had now deposited Johnson safely back in Edinburgh and was also taking an interest in Mr Thorpe's education programme. He tumbled to it immediately—well, probably it wasn't the first time.

'Poor old Isaac Newton,' he explained to Frank, 'just because he had the misfortune to go to Trinity. I'm afraid he isn't held in very high regard around this table. Not to be compared to our own college hero, Josiah Wentworth.' And Simon gestured across at a picture behind Sir Barry. A fat Elizabethan gentleman looking vacant and bored.

Frank now felt completely lost. 'Josiah Wentworth . . . ? Was he in the same class as Newton?'

'Far better. Echelons higher.' Simon Jeffrey gave a superior conspiratorial smile. More a smirk.

'But I've never heard of him,' Frank protested. (And I did do two semesters of History of Science at Harvard. No, that was better left unsaid.)

'Ah no, that's the point,' Simon added triumphantly, as if everything should now be totally clear.

Plates were being collected. New hot silver dishes. Pheasant. Brussels sprouts. Cauliflower in a sauce that could be a meal on its own. No potatoes, nothing so crude. Twenty-year-old Burgundy poured into the second of the five glasses before each place.

Frank shook her head, partly to reassure herself that she still had one. Long blond hair cascading over the black academic gown which Lord Johns had thoughtfully provided. 'Oh but you must, my dear. They are de rigeur at a Feast.' And now it *was* getting hot.

The Master decided he had spent enough time being chatty to old moneybags. Turned to his right. Took a long steady look at Frank. Which she returned, with equal candour.

'Just admiring your pulchritude, my dear.'

That made him the fourth person that day to have called Frank 'my dear'. Well, she thought, I suppose this is *dear* old England. Grin and bear it. And *this* is the man who's supposed to clue me in on the emergency? This drink-sodden old frump!

Frank resisted the temptation to ask whether Josiah Wentworth was a virgin too. Or what possible relevance that had to scientific fame. 'What did he—', she chose the word with care, 'what did Josiah Wentworth—er—discover?'

Linguist manqué and woolly organiser, even Dr Most's friends had to concede that. He had been a compromise candidate for the Mastership. No one's first choice but no one really objected to him. Sixtyish but hair still black—he just doesn't worry, Frank supposed to herself. And he knew a bit about everyone. Lord Johns trusted him and at lunch that day had informed Frank, still dazed from the Atlantic crossing, that Patrick Most would be the only person to be told of her mission. 'After all, if Patrick vouches for you, you'll be accepted into college life. Freedom to operate, don't you know. And I'm sure Patrick wouldn't pinch any state secrets. Wouldn't know what to do with them, what!'

Frank wasn't too sure. In her experience it was the most unlikely person who could turn out to be villain. But since it was Lord Johns who had hired her services, on behalf of Her Majesty's Government—'Purely informal you realise. We'd deny having anything to do with you if anything—er—happened. Although of course the agreed fee would still be paid.' Since Lord Johns called the tune he could presumably let who he wanted in on Frank's true identity. And, it turned out, Dr Most had already been informed.

'Discover? No, he didn't actually discover anything.' The Master didn't seem quite as certain as Simon Jeffrey that this was a good thing, but he was putting a good face on it. 'You see, Newton really struck lucky. He just happened to work in a field where there were discoveries ready to be made, you could say. I mean, gravitation, it was just waiting to be uncovered. Asking, one might say. And optics and all that.'

Most's voice tailed off as he again looked Frank in the eye. Young enough to be his daughter. But maturity. Style, that was the word. You had to hand it to these Americans. . . . He took another long draught of Burgundy. Detached a leaf of a Brussels sprout and conveyed it gingerly to his mouth.

It didn't seem terribly important but Frank felt that if she couldn't get this much clear there wasn't going to be much hope of working out who was trying to steal information on the Kavendish's Pasar breakthrough and sell it—for a handsome sum, no doubt—to the Chinese. That is, if Her Majesty's Government's worst suspicions, as conveyed to her by Lord Johns, were well enough founded.

'What did he *do* then? What was Josiah Wentworth famous for, Dr Most?' Frank put on her most imploring look and hoped the Master was not too sozzled to be, at least momentarily, melted.

'Ah yes, do.' Another leaf, and a modest sip of wine. 'Well, he didn't actually do anything. And he isn't famous. I mean, is he? Had you heard of him before?' There seemed a pathetic current of hope in Most's question.

Ye gods, thought Frank, I feel I'm living life backwards. But, luckily, the Master just continued: 'No, he was a thinker. Not very fashionable, then or now. But the few of us, Fellows of this college, who have studied his writings—all unpublished, you understand—feel that we have come into contact with a great mind. Well, if not exactly a *great* mind . . . great *mind* . . .'

Most seemed unable to decide which word should be pronounced more emphatically. He appeared to be mouthing them to himself and then gradually relapsed into silence. Frank could swear that the picture of Wentworth shuddered a little. It was hard to decide whether in pride or dissent. Or perhaps it just felt like a fidget.

James Thorpe again claimed the Master's attention. There was the question of what the new wing should be called, Frank heard. Who it should be named after. The Master tentatively suggested Hervey de Stanton, founder of Michaelhouse back in 1324. 'He was Chancellor of the Exchequer and a Canon of Baths and Wells,' Mr Thorpe was told, as Sir Barry nodded vigorously. But—surely even Most and Stone could see—

James Thorpe plainly intended his own name to go on what his money bought.

Simon Jeffrey was now preoccupied with the red-haired intense man sitting opposite Frank. The distinct Yorkshire accent seemed at odds with Simon's languorous insouciance. 'The hook shot can be highly dangerous unless done by a real expert.' But at least he seemed to put more enthusiasm into explaining the niceties of cricket than had been spared for Sam Johnson's travels.

Explaining cricket? To a Russian? Dr Leon Ivanovitch, brilliant physicist who had so spoken his mind that he had simply been dismissed from his post as Director of the Soviet Nuclear Research Institute. Forced irrevocably to leave his fatherland and work with Barry Stone at the Kavendish. Leon Ivanovitch was not impressed. 'But how can you watch any game that goes on for five days? You must go to sleep. No intelligent person could do otherwise.'

The first sitting of undergraduates were now leaving the hall. Twos and threes, deep in conversation. A mere sprinkling of girls, admitted for the first time just eight months before, after 650 years of male territorialism. Most of the men wore neat dark suits and ties but a few had simply neck-high sweaters, although they too sported gowns.

The Master broke off long enough to answer Frank's question. Objectively and succinctly, which made a change. 'They used to, indeed they used to. Until last year. A jacket and tie were obligatory for dinner. Then we admitted females.' The Master plainly approved of women. But in their place. And although he wasn't one to rock the boat of progress there were clearly reservations as to whether this was one of the right places. 'We couldn't make the girls wear a jacket and tie so some of the men said why should they? Spirit of equality, you know.'

Patrick Most shook his head, with slightly puckered eyebrows that said I-told-you-no-good-would-come-of-it, before resuming the debate with his current philanthropist on why a flat roof was absolutely essential for Thorpe Court, even though everything else in sight was pointed or domed.

Again left to her own thoughts, Frank went over the lunch with Lord Johns in that stuffy dining room off St James's. She really had been the only woman in the room—apart from waitresses. Also probably the only person under fifty. The Delta flight from Atlanta had been an hour late and it hadn't seemed to occur to his Lordship that what she really needed was a shower and a couple of hours of rest. The English, of course, don't rest in the middle of the day. Simply because it is 'not done'.

Frank le Roux, investigator extraordinary. Toast of the governments and big corporations over five continents. People whose puzzles she had unlocked during the preceding half-dozen years. Despair of the men on whom she selectively bestowed her caresses. Frank le Roux, natural great-granddaughter of Buddy Bolden, black cornet player who blew so hard in the early days of jazz in New Orleans that his brain went zing! But not before he had inspired Louis the Armstrong and really, Frank considered, set music right on course for the twentieth century.

She was still registered as doctoral candidate at the University of Chicago. But detective work was so much more—well, gripping—than sociology. Still, that would do as a cover, Lord Johns had decided. Frank could pretend to be engaged on a study of interpersonal relationships in academic life. Say that she'd already done field work at Berkeley and Yale. What more natural than to come to Cambridge? The Kavendish laboratory. And Michaelhouse College, principally because it housed the three members of the Pasar team. Lord Johns enunciated it in a breathy whisper, forefinger raised as if to close off his lips after the *m* of *team*, perhaps to stop the phrase escaping again.

There was Sir Barry Stone, leader of the group. 'We believe this may be a breakthrough of the same order as splitting the atom at the old Cavendish, fifty-odd years ago,' Lord Johns had remarked, 'although old Barry couldn't really be put in the same class as Rutherford. He has a good team, that's one of the secrets. Leon Ivanovitch, one of the most outstanding minds in science. Leon is totally anti-Soviet now. All for us. Really, that's why he had to leave Russia, I suppose.'

The lunchtime cigar smoke in his Lordship's club had been

overpowering to jet-lagged Frank. Seemed to percolate into her orange juice, into the trout. Lord Johns hadn't been offended that she'd declined to partake of his bottle of claret. Probably, Frank decided, put it down to her being a woman, or an American, or an investigator.

'And then there's Sampson Ndagbera. From Nigeria. Still doing his PhD but really one of the key minds in the whole project. Highly reliable fellow they say. The British influence is still very strong in Nigeria, you know.'

The point of the whole exercise, Frank gradually gleaned, the reason she had been summoned from New Orleans at two days' notice, was the range of application of Pasars. It had taken a dozen years after the atom was split to realise that atomic energy could be used to blast mankind off the face of its planet. This time the consequences had been foreseen even before anything had been published. Which was why perhaps nothing would be published. Ever. Or at least that was how the privileged policy-makers in Her Majesty's Government saw it.

'Imagine something rather similar in construction to a child's clockwork motor but with the potency of a power station.' Lord Johns knew no more about physics than Frank. 'Barry feels it may be the first step towards faster-than-light travel. Could get someone to another star in a matter of weeks. Or days.' If one didn't know too much about something, no point in half-measures, Lord Johns seemed to believe, and Frank rather agreed.

The Head of the Home Office had poured himself a third glass of claret, sipped, spilt a little across his two chins and wiped them off, patting the dribbles with a starched napkin. 'The applications of Pasars are almost incredible—unlimited power at negligible cost. Heating homes, running cars and planes, Barry thinks. At one stroke it'll solve half the problems we now have in the world.'

Yeah, yeah, Frank decided not to say out loud. Solve most of the problems of the rich nations all right. How to get from one golf-course to another as quickly as possible. But what of famine, oppression, the sheer misery of the other half of the world? Still, this wasn't what she'd been hired to worry about. Better concentrate on the task ahead.

'And of course,' His Lordship continued, 'the possibilities of misuse are just as colossal. There's not the shadow of a doubt that a Pasar bomb would make our present armoury look like a cupboard of cap pistols.'

So, he continued, the secret was to remain in Britain. America knew something of what was going on, and they had agreed it was best for the major powers not to be let in on Pasar development, at least for the time being. Russia and China had been told nothing. But—and this was the cause for panic—intelligence sources in China reported that something was known. Indeed, that bits of the puzzle were being smuggled out of Cambridge, little by little.

'Couldn't they work it out for themselves?' Frank wondered. 'After all, calculus was invented simultaneously by two people in different countries. Or was it algebra?'

'Indeed they are trying to.' Lord Johns sipped his coffee while Frank attacked a rather fine ice-cream. Praline flavour. Made her feel half-way human again. 'The Americans have about six teams working on it.'

'But,' he leaned across the table, as if to avoid being overheard by the fat admirals and brigadiers and captains of industry who slouched over neighbouring tables. 'They tell me that this isn't the sort of thing which can be got at by hard work. Apparently Sampson Ndagbera more-or-less dreamt of a certain equation. And it worked. One in a million chance. No logical reason for it, not that we can understand in our present state of science, that is.'

'But if the Chinese have got the equation,' Frank protested, 'it all seems a bit late.'

'No, no, no, on the contrary.' Lord Johns replaced the cup and consulted a gold hunting watch on his fob. (Or at least Frank thought that was what it was called.) 'They tell me it's not a simple equation like $e=mc^2$. About 200 pages you need and if one is missing then all the rest are useless. A wonderfully simple product, but deuced complex theory behind it all. Anyway the

Chinese would need all 200 pages. They may have some of them. The reason we've called you in, Miss le Roux, is to stop them getting the rest.'

Lord Johns' chauffeur hadn't looked Chinese—in fact he looked more like a large pugilistic bodyguard than a chauffeur. But he'd been given the rest of the day off for 'security reasons'. His Lordship steered the Mercedes past St Paul's and Tower Bridge before negotiating the slow, seamy East End and then driving up the motorway in forty-five minutes.

Security at the Kavendish was good, he assured Frank, but the Prime Minister wasn't satisfied. Apparently her husband had connections with IBM, who had hired Frank the previous winter to put a stop to a gigantic swindle that involved putting dummy symbols into a lot of individual user programs and then simultaneously triggering them all off during a share-time period. It just meant that each program appeared to take ten per cent longer to run than it should and there was that much time available for free-lance work the ingenious programmers accepted at seventy-five per cent of normal rates. And seventy-five per cent of ten per cent of the budget of even one large IBM installation provided a handy nest-egg.

'I'm told your methods are—ah—unusual,' Lord Johns had commented as he ignored a NO ENTRY sign into Trinity Street. 'And also effective.' He let his own opinion of Frank's engagement show through for just a moment. 'And I suppose no harm can come of it.' The Prime Minister's will be done.

Frank was jerked back into the reality of the Feast for the Apparition of St Michael. She remembered it from the minute details of religious ritual to which her mother had always attended. Apparently some long-forgotten alumnus had provided a bequest for Fellows and their guests to gorge themselves to the utmost on this day each year. The undergraduates, in the hall below the raised platform on which Frank now sat, had 'commons' (whatever that was) as usual. The remains of pheasant was being cleared away on high, and bulky crêpes stuffed with seafood placed before each festive diner.

The second sitting of undergraduates had each been provided

with a plate of soup by ordinary waiters, less splendidly attired than he who again replenished the Master's glass (and fetched Frank a tumbler of iced water without even a grimace of disapproval). Suddenly the students all stood, picked up their bowls of soup and walked in single file, slow march, out of the hall. Before the last row had begun to move the first batch were back, grinning, each now holding an empty plate.

'Oh lawd, not again,' the Master sighed to Sir Barry. Then, realising that James Thorpe and Frank required some commentary on what might appear to be yet another ancient custom: 'They go and empty their soup in the pond, out there in the Court. Happens about once a month. Just because we're having a bit of a feast. Silly sort of prank. Killed all the goldfish in the pond last time.'

Simon Jeffrey was now talking to Andrew Delaney, Professor of Pure Mathematics, who sat opposite him at the end of the table. He was someone else who knew about Project Pasar, Lord Johns had mentioned. Checked up on the proof of an important theorem, since he was one of Ndagbera's supervisors. Didn't know the whole story but he did have a fair bit of it. And plenty of opportunity for nosing out the rest, Frank reflected. She had never trusted people who appeared to be quite so absent-mindedly professorish. As she watched, Delaney picked up the empty Moselle glass in apparent error. Drank nothing from it and then put it down again, licking his lips, before taking a real sip from the new wine that had come along with the crêpes. Sallow face, vague eyes, already two red stains across the brocade of his dress shirt. Façade? Well, it shouldn't be too hard to uncover.

The undergraduates now seemed to be quite happily eating cottage pie and carrots. Apparently there wasn't any custom of taking that out and strewing it all over the lawn. Frank suddenly found herself the object of amused attention from Dr Ivanovitch, across the table. 'A penny for your thoughts, Miss le Roux. Or should it be one quarter-dollar, making allowance for capitalist inflationary tendencies?'

Leon's sing-song yet astringent English, stresses consistently misplaced, contrasted with Frank's warm southern timbres. 'I was just thinking what a small world it is. Last night I ate in the Gumbo Shop, on St Peter Street in New Orleans. And now it's like going back in a time machine. All these black ties and pretty shirts. And—' Frank gestured at the pictures hanging behind the Master and James Thorpe, 'those guys must have lived when Louisiana still belonged to the Indians.'

'Indeed, yes.' Professor Delaney took it upon himself proudly to identify John Fisher, Master of Michaelhouse in the late fifteenth century and notable university reformer. 'Then the large portrait is Hervey de Stanton, our founder, you know.'

Delaney's cultivated accent, each vowel carefully and deliberately rounded, contrasted with Jeffrey's Yorkshire inflexions that he believed went with his self-image as enfant terrible of the Eng. Lit. establishment. 'Ay, but tha shouldna talk of pictures ont' wall, Andrew lad. Tha knows the rules of hall, doesn't tha?'

Leon Ivanovitch hastened to explain, as a relative newcomer who had—with a certain amount of effort—assimilated the local social constraints. 'There are things one does not talk of at dinner. The pictures on the wall. Work. Ladies—oh, that was last year. I do not know what has happened to the rule now that they are—how is it said?—entered here themselves.'

'Admitted,' Frank supplied. 'But what on earth do you talk of, then?'

'Ah,' Leon leaned across the table as if it were an especially juicy piece of gossip. 'Most evenings the oldest Fellow present reminisces about what the college was like in his younger days. That is why I so seldom eat here myself. The first three or four times, quite interesting. But then I know it. One night I think I tell it to them myself but the Master did not seem—' Leon hesitated over the word, '—expressed?'

'Impressed,' Frank once again supplied.

He busied himself with disposing of large forkfuls of prawn and oyster and calamari and pancake. Not a handsome man, Frank decided. Brilliant red hair, crooked nose, blotchy red complexion. Somehow Leon contrived to look scruffy in a dinner-jacket—tie not quite straight, one cuff showing and the other not. He'd look more at home in a windcheater and jeans, haversack on his back, about to scale a mountain or explore some dangerous pothole.

But his humour, intelligence and compassion shone through, somehow out of place among the stolid solemnities of Michaelhouse High Table. Leon Ivanovitch was surely a man who could make a brilliant discovery. He'd have the style and insight to project his applications, no doubt at all. And the idealism and courage to sneak it to the Chinese? Why not. Maybe he saw there a chance for the true practice of Marxism, something that had so blatantly failed in the Soviet Union.

Leon now began to tell a joke. (Of course he would!) It gave Frank a chance to look down at the far end of the table. She'd been introduced to everyone, very briefly, before dinner.

'There is a contrast between porter and professor in Cambridge college,' Leon began.

Lord Johns sat at the very end of the table. Frank had been told that, as an Honorary Fellow, he came up mostly for Feasts. What was his role in all this? The lunch conversation hadn't rung totally true. Could they really keep a discovery as important as Pasars from the rest of the world? The British plainly thought they could. No longer a major power, with the potential to threaten others, they still cherished a role as self-appointed international arbiter, upholder of decency and honour. No—even Lord Johns must have another side to him.

'The porter knew a little bit about lots of things. While the professor knew a great deal about just a few things,' Leon continued, with gusto, pausing now for a gentle drink (he had wine still in all three glasses).

Opposite Sir Barry's upright figure was Louise Bates, petite President of the Cambridge Union. This was, Frank had been informed, a debating society and social club. Very, very prestigious, tended to be a good source of Prime Ministers and suchlike. Women had only been admitted recently and Louise was in fact the first American woman to be President. She had a degree in physics from Vassar and was now doing another BA here. In between public appearances, that was. Louise's three glasses were all dry and she was now telling Mr Thorpe—in a brassy New England voice that was certainly too loud for the occasion—how car rentals were *so* much more efficient in the States.

Next to Louise sat Sampson Ndagbera. Surely the key figure. I mean, Frank reflected, why don't the Chinese just kidnap him and they'd have the whole caboodle. Sampson had sat quite silent, certainly since the soup procession. Slowly chewing, drinking from the single tall glass of orange juice that had been waiting at his place. Thinking. Dreaming up a new equation? Or comparing a Michaelhouse Feast with famine in eastern Nigeria?

'So the porter got to know less and less about more and more. And the professor learnt more and more about less and less. Until finally the porter knew nothing about everything. And the professor everything about nothing.' Leon turned to his right, to Bernice Dodds, Reader in Anthropology, current mistress of the Master. And she did laugh, a cool bell-like tinkle. A polite laugh, a genuine laugh. Her mouth opened, daintily, as she laughed, but the corners didn't turn up.

The second sitting of undergraduates had now finished the apple pie and custard and departed. A tray of small dishes of lemon sorbet was brought in to the Feast. 'Quite a restrained dessert,' Frank remarked to Leon, only to be immediately corrected from her right. 'No, no. This is just to clean out your stomach, make it ready for the main course.' But I thought we'd had the main course, Frank just stopped herself saying to Simon.

Now it did come. Roast turkey, chipolatas, stuffing, peas, courgettes. And there were potatoes. The English always have potatoes. Gentle slivers, in a sour cream sauce. A real wine now, the Master informed everybody. Nuits-St-Georges, 1933. Needs to be drunk up—in fact it might have been at its peak last year. Sir Barry nodded in agreement and Mr Thorpe grunted—it could have been in disbelief or pleasure or just contempt. Only Lord Johns muttered to Louise Bates: 'five years ago more like it.'

Dr Bernice Dodds, sitting opposite the Master, clinked her

glass against his. It seemed an anachronism, almost an obscene gesture, in that setting. Bernice Dodds was in fact the only Michaelhouse Fellow Frank had heard of prior to the detailed briefing Lord Johns had provided on the drive up.

Surely the whole world knew the author of *Primitive Procreation*? Why hadn't anyone before Bernice had the idea of putting together a survey of sexual habits across the non-civilised people of the world? It was rumoured that she had herself tried out a fair few of the uncomfortable-sounding positions described, during lengthy periods of anthropological field-work in the jungles of Africa and South America and the deserts of Australia.

Yet the main reason Bernice was such a sought-after guest on talk shows, on the frequent occasions she crossed the Atlantic, was that she was so proto-typically English. Attractive, yes. Sexy, well yes. But her impeccable English manner, and the cool, well-modulated, Cambridge accent. They simply threw the American audience, to hear such a voice describe fornication in the forest, and copulation deep in the Congo, not to mention what it was like having it off with a subincised man in the Gibson desert. It wasn't that Bernice ever really said anything very explicit. But she hinted and raised her eyebrows, which was enough to double viewing figures whenever Dr Dodds was on the box. And the reason the feast was being held more than two weeks after the actual date of St Michael's apparition, Frank had been told, was because the Master had delayed it for Bernice's return from her latest trip.

Hard to tell Bernice's age. Must be forty. She gave Frank a no-nonsense look as her hand inadvertently brushed Most's when they went at the same time for a salt cellar. 'Each guest has his own condiments at a feast.' Bernice pointed out the cruet set ranged in a neat crystal trough before Frank.

A sudden bang. Something missing between Louise and Bernice. A gap. Sampson Ndagbera slumped over his turkey, hand outstretched across the table, the glass it had held dribbling orange juice into the lap of James Thorpe, near-illiterate multi-millionaire.

The mathematical genius didn't look dead or anything, but

surely, thought Frank, a certain amount of consternation should be in order. Delaney and Jeffrey didn't even look up from their argument about whether Sobers was a greater all-rounder than Botham.

Two waiters pulled out Ndagbera's chair, one of them supporting his head, and then carried him off into the combination room. Bernice actually folded a hand across the recumbent body. Sir Barry assured Mr Thorpe that the stain would come off his dress trousers, bought specially for the occasion. Lord Johns lit a cigar and appeared to blow smoke after the departing genius. Only Leon Ivanovitch seemed concerned by the incident, bustling around, opening the door and following into the combination room to see that Sampson was properly arranged on a couch, a window opened near him.

'Poor old Sampson,' Dr Most drawled, roughly in Frank's direction. 'Always happens. Well, almost always. Will come along to Feasts, the dear chap, but he will pass out like that.' Frank would have liked to enquire whether it was due to the heat, or some medical condition, or sheer boredom. But the incident was already completely forgotten. Bernice and Louise appeared to have edged their chairs a little closer. There was scarcely a trace of where Sampson had been a couple of minutes earlier.

Frank jumped at a peculiar rasping sound from the direction of an oddly-placed balcony down the left side of the hall. Then something that sounded like a lute being plucked. A violin and a lute?

Leon was watching in amusement. 'Decadent capitalist custom' didn't fully inform Frank. It was left to Delaney, more as an aside. 'At last. Should be serenaded all through a Feast, always used to be. But those bally students started hissing up at the musicians' gallery so now one has to wait until they've chomped their chops and departed.' He opened his mouth so wide and so long on the *aaa* of *departed* that Frank almost mistook it for a yawn.

Delaney and Jeffrey settled down again to review form for the newly commenced cricket season. Mr Thorpe quite adamantly informed Most and Stone that he wanted yellow bricks on top of each doorway, to make them more visible at night.

Alone of the company, it seemed, Leon wanted to find out more about Frank. Her slightly olive skin which blended into the long rust-coloured dress; dangling coral earrings that shimmered like the cut-glass chandelier. He asked plainly: 'I see you belong to a minority group, Miss le Roux, as I do.'

'Well, yes.' Having discovered the condiment tray Frank couldn't resist playing with it, trying to balance a squared-off jar of salt on top of the squat pepper pot. It was good to be direct but there was still some residual anxiety about the topic, a relic of generations of shame and despair. 'Sure I'm black. On mother's side.' One-eighth part, no less. 'And maybe a few more ancestors. Most people in New Orleans are pretty mixed.'

'Ah, New Orleans.' Leon Ivanovitch drooled the words. 'That is where I dream to go. American jazz, it is my favourite pastime. In Russia I have records but they are left behind. Now I buy all over again. King Oliver, that was the greatest band of all time.'

Wow, Frank decided. One thing I must remember is not to let on about great-grandfather Buddy B. or Dr Leon will give me no peace at all. Once, in Tokyo, she had unwisely let drop her parentage and three earnest jazz fans had literally followed Frank everywhere she went. Waited outside her hotel in the morning, bought her meals, tickets to the theatre. She'd just had to leave before suffocating.

But this, most decidely, wasn't what HMG had hired Frank for. 'Tell me, Dr Ivanovitch, don't you miss your Research Institute in Moscow? I mean, the Kavendish is good but you're, er . . .' Not the boss, well it wouldn't quite do to spell it out with the boss himself, Sir Barry Stone, within earshot. Even if he did appear now to be fully preoccupied with red and green brick-work.

The Russian smiled in understanding. 'Do call me Leon.' He had a think. Took another sip of wine. The musicians launched into another madrigal, gentle music that suited the mousse which had now appeared. 'It is a good team here.' Ivanovitch looked down at where Ndagbera had sat. 'I have learnt more and done more in a short time than was possible in Moscow.'

There was plainly more to come. Frank waited. Pasars could not be mentioned, but a hint perhaps. Leon's thoughts, though, ran in a different direction. 'In Moscow I had trouble. Because I am Jewish. It is hard to know what effect that had. And because of my life-style. The KGB, they were always inquisitive. And although I had a good job, fine salary by Moscow standards, I was never allowed in the University. They considered that I was not reliable enough to have contact with students.'

Frank was momentarily distracted by Bernice. Louise had been talking about physics, the excitement of pure science, the possibility of discovery and proof and prediction. Then something had been said which made Bernice snap angrily at her. Louise sat frozen, reddened, then took a quick gulp of wine, appeared to choke, turned towards Lord Johns who patted her firmly on the back. Bernice spoke to the Master, a peremptory tone such as no wife would have dared assume. Most beckoned the head waiter.

Leon's story was not dull. 'I have a friend who is Professor of Physics. They ask me to give a seminar and the only way is to have it Saturday night. Students may invite friends in for social intercourse so he tells them to invite me. Three hours we are permitted and I give seminar. It was the only way.'

The waiter appeared with—if that were possible—more solemnity than before. Progressed slowly along the platform and deposited a golden chalice before the Master. All ten of the festive diners stood. By some hidden sign the musicians stopped, in mid-madrigal.

Most picked up the ancient vessel, reverently, by its two handles. Incanted some Latin, Frank presumed. Not exactly mumbled, more like a loud mutter. Bowed three times to Mr James Thorpe who bowed three times in return. Mr Thorpe accepted the potation, drank from it as if he had been long deprived of liquor, turned to Sir Barry Stone, repeated the same Latin, word perfect, and bowed. Sir Barry bowed back the requisite three times.

And so it went on. The musicians began again, this time an ancient drinking song. Sir Barry to Lord Johns. Bow, recite magical formula, drink.

Patrick Most turned to Frank: 'Wonderful fellow, Ffothergill-Hawthorn-Williams. Gave us this feast, you know. Very munificent bequest. In the eighteenth century I recall. Or was it the sixteenth? Yes, very possibly.'

Frank thought it might be polite to ask a little about the antecedents of Michaelhouse. Rich benefactors might become hazy but . . . 'Tell me about St Michael, Dr Most. What was he canonised for?'

The chalice went now to Louise as Patrick Most tittered at Frank's faux pas. 'He was no mortal, my dear.' I suppose I *will* get used to it eventually, Frank determined. 'An archangel. Fierce warrior. Gave Moses the tablets on top of that mountain, you know. And—' the Master contrived to appear mysterious, 'he knew the word.' It was said with a reverent, deliberate expulsion of breath, as if he had been announcing 'the Queen'.

Bernice now had the golden vessel. Surely it must remind her of some primitive custom, the precursor to a bacchanalian revel in a forgotten corner of Africa. Frank speculated for a moment on what might happen if Bernice were suddenly to shed her clothes and dance naked on the table. Crushing individual cruet sets with a steely heel while shaking her crotch eagerly at Mr James Thorpe, inviting him to consummate the two-million-dollar benefaction there and then, yellow bricks or no yellow bricks.

And here was Frank supposed to be guarding the secret of Project Pasar. How was that to be done? One man at Michaelhouse knew her mission. The Master. Vague, ineffectual, fussy. But he also knew about Project Pasar. How? Why? A linguist, Lord Johns had said.

'What word?' Not to have responded thus would have been the height of rudeness.

'Well,' continued the Master, as the potion passed now to Leon Ivanovitch who greatly enjoyed the ceremony, bowing very low and drinking deliberately and deeply with a satisfying 'aaah' at the excellence of whatever ancient recipe was deserving of such deference.

'I'm glad you asked,' Most responded appreciately. 'No one knows the exact word, of course. But the Book of Enoch, chapter fifty-nine, tells us there *was* a secret word. God used it to make the earth, that's how important it was.'

'You don't say.' Frank had been exposed to a great deal of Bible but very little Apocrypha. She wasn't sure if this might not be some subtle in-group English joke. The chalice had now moved on to Professor Delaney, and Frank was getting a little concerned about the Latin mumbo-jumbo.

'Oh yes, it's all there in Enoch. That magic word first of all made the heavens strong. Sort-of implying that they might have been a bit dithery at the time. Then founded the earth upon the water. Made the sun and moon complete their orbits—can you imagine them just skating around all over the place before that? And then it made water and wind, and thunder and lightning, and hail and hoar-frost and mist and rain and . . .'

Simon Jeffrey now turned to Frank. It sounded like 'obis-kwi-no-bis-kwi-sanctos-haminos-Ffothergill-Hawthorn-Williams.' Frank's short-term memory held on to the succession of syllables like a limpet. Jeffrey bowed thrice. Frank bowed three times (such is the difference between the English and American languages, and customs).

Frank, with chalice clasped in both hands. It needed to be. Heavy. Drink! Just the merest sip would be enough.

Crash. As if the roof had fallen in. No, not the roof, the large gilt-framed portrait of Hervey de Stanton. Fallen from its hook to the floor, bounced, twice, started to settle on the floor, face-down.

Utmost consternation. Frank placed the chalice carefully on the table as every Feast guest seemed to rush past her to view the damage. Delicately upturn old Hervey. It did take four people to lift the founder's picture. The cord had broken. Cord? Should have been golden wire, surely.

Dinner, apparently, couldn't go on until King Edward's Chancellor of the Exchequer was back on his hook. Tie the cord. 'Here, let me do it, used to be a Girl Scout.' Louise Bates. Always an American to the rescue.

Frank walked towards the picture of Josiah Wentworth, secret genius. He looked more like a debt-collector.

What a contrast with the unremarked collapse of Sampson Ndagbera, mathematical wonder-child, brain behind Project Pasar. It must have been fifteen minutes before Hervey was back in position, two or three inches higher by virtue of the shorter cord. But level. No worse for wear. And now he could oversee the completion of the festive toast.

Frank suddenly realised, as everyone else stood at their places and looked at her, that she must now grasp the golden bowl, recite the mystic oath, and bow to the Master. What oath? It had completely gone. Well, there was only one thing to do. Follow family tradition and improvise. 'Glabus scrintus, homines fantus, glabus rex,' Frank intoned, a shade triumphantly, and then remembered to add: 'Ffothergill-Hawthorn-Williams.' She bowed to the Master, who smiled. (Well at least it rhymed, Frank thought defiantly, which is more than you can say of the original.) Dr Most bowed. As he began to take his draught of the precious potion, Frank remembered that she hadn't touched it herself. Too bad, and too late. She conjured up a brew of rosemary and squashed beetles, sarsaparilla, ground alligator teeth, and blood taken from the lobes of tieless undergraduates—as a sort of mental consolation.

The golden chalice was carried off, still rather full, and everyone sat down to fruit and cheese, which must have been placed on the table while Hervey was having his tantrum.

Sir Barry Stone leant back to speak with Frank behind the backs of Thorpe and Most. 'Lord Johns was just telling me that you're here to study how people get on together in a lab. The Kavendish. Very glad to have you. Although—' his voice suddenly became less inviting, '—we've a fair amount of security just now. Rather special project.'

Stone glanced across the table at a black figure. Frank saw with surprise that Sampson was again seated between Louise and Bernice. Cracking nuts with what looked like a silver clamp, as if he'd never been away. Must have returned during the picture hanging, Frank supposed.

'Yes, Sir Barry. Ah'd be really grateful for any help you can provide.' Without meaning it, Frank's vowels had taken on a more southern, Tennessee-Williams timbre. 'Ah've heard so much about your wonderful laboratory. Back when Ah was a student at Haavaad.'

'Oh!' This combination seemed to catch Sir Barry off balance. Then: 'How about breakfast tomorrow? Nine o'clock, staircase E, room seven? Tell me what I can do for you then, eh.'

Frank had no time to reply. The figure between them seemed to convulse, and make a sound like a gargle. The Master straightened once and then slumped forward in his chair, head banging into a bowl of serrated pineapple rings and peeled grapes. Bernice screamed. Lord Johns, who it turned out had some sort of medical training, moved purposefully around the table.

A first idea that this was some Cambridge disease or habit. But, unlike the Ndagbera swoon, Most's appeared unexpected. Everyone stared, open-mouthed, at the recumbent Master. And at Lord Johns.

Come off it, thought Frank. This man who is to be my Pasar guide. Has he fainted? Or collapsed from a surfeit of food? Or from innumerable glasses of Moselle, and Burgundy, and claret, and gold-chaliced potion, and now—with the fruit—cold tingling hock?

No. None of these. From death. Cold, tingling death.

II

'THERE IS ABSOLUTELY no doubt at all. None. So the police tell me.'

Frank was sitting on the very edge of a hard, wooden chair. An old chair, made for ascetic monastic bums. Nine thirty in the morning. No sunshine came through Sir Barry Stone's latticed bay window. Grey English clouds covered the sky.

Frank had left the hall immediately after Dr Patrick Most, Master of Michaelhouse College, had been declared totally and irrevocably dead. Gone to her room at the top of a dull brown staircase. Closed windows. Changed from formal festive gown into black tights, and danced to the jangled rock cavalcade on Radio One. Danced and thought, what was she doing here? What had she been hired to do? What melodrama was unfolding in this mediaeval citadel? Frank felt that she was entirely the wrong person to protect the secrets of Project Pasar from slit-eyed spies. Witches and dragons and horny-handed goblins seemed much more appropriate.

'Most was poisoned. An oxalate derivative. Would have acted faster if he hadn't—er—eaten so much.'

Frank hadn't been certain about the breakfast appointment. Surely, in the circumstances. . . . But when she knocked, hesitantly, on the door of room E7 at fifteen minutes after nine o'clock, Sir Barry Stone was sitting expectantly, sipping coffee. Grapefruit. Kippers kept hot over a small flame. Toast and Dundee marmalade.

The head of the Kavendish looked a little tired. As Senior Fellow he had been up most of the night 'helping the police with their investigations'. But still routine went on. A breakfast engagement should be kept, the homicidal poisoning of one's Master notwithstanding.

Country boy from Goondiwindi, an obscure little town on the south Queensland border, Barry Stone had supported himself through university in Brisbane. Got a Rhodes Scholarship, *the* Queensland Rhodes Scholarship. Worked around the older institutions in England and then naturally gravitated to Rutherford's old job, head of the premier scientific laboratory in the world. That it had been, beyond question, in the 'twenties and 'thirties. And now? Well, if Project Pasar lived up to one-quarter of Lord Johns' description, Barry Stone could name the year he preferred to collect the Nobel Prize.

Thirty years in England had provided the thinnest veneer of sophistication. He still looked like a farm boy, a farm boy with a high forehead and piercing, questioning blue eyes. A manner not as blunt as Leon Ivanovitch but straightforward, no nonsense. Frank felt an instinctive rapport, an outgoing warmth. If only the news Barry had to impart had been more wholesome.

'Tests clearly show that the festive toast was poisoned. The chalice was still half full, in the kitchen, and it had a lethal dose. No one could have taken a sip and survived.'

Frank stopped in the middle of trying to separate a piece of dry kipper flesh from bone on one side and crinkly skin on the other. Put fork and knife down. Stared at Sir Barry, as he continued eating. The words slowly penetrated her half-awake brain.

'But everyone had drunk out of the cup—goblet, whatever you call it. So the poison must have been . . . must have been . . .'

'Precisely. It could only have been put into the toast while the portrait was being rehung. You put the chalice on the table, as I recall, and walked away. So there was plenty of opportunity for anyone to tamper with it.'

Frank thought, and shivered. 'Yes, everyone was rushing around. And attention was on the picture. Anyone could have tipped—some powder, was it?' Stone nodded. 'Into the cup.'

Frank tried again to eat salty fish. Turned to Sir Barry to find him regarding her. Sympathetically? 'Do the police have any suspicions?'

'None. They have ten names.' Stone still retained the Australian vowel, making this word sound like 'nimes'. 'You, James

Thorpe, Delaney, Simon Jeffrey, Ivanovitch, Dr Dodds.' Was it Frank's imagination, or had there been a sour edge to his pronunciation of the name of the best-known anthropologist in England? 'Me, Lord Johns, Louise Bates. And the waiters of course,' Sir Barry concluded as if they didn't have names at all. And then added: 'And Sampson. He came back just then. Went past the goblet. Ideal opportunity.'

'But surely . . .' Frank protested.

'But surely none of us would have done it? But actually one of us did.'

Frank realised that Stone had taken upon himself what should be—what normally would be—her role. Looking at the evidence objectively, eliminating possibilities, deducing. Better pull myself together a bit. Stop being foxed by this eminent antipodean charmer. (Old enough to be my father. Well, so what?)

'If the murderer wanted to get the Master this was an ideal chance. And he just happened to have a paperful of poison in his pocket in case the opportunity arose. Oh look, Sir Barry, this is ridiculous!'

'It's what happened,' he reminded her.

'So,' Frank thought aloud. 'When the picture fell down this was the perfect opportunity. Everyone had drunk from the chalice except Dr Most.'

'And you,' Stone told her, quite simply. 'I'm an experimental scientist. Trained to observe. And to remember. You hadn't drunk when the picture fell, and you didn't drink afterwards. You're the only one who didn't.'

'That means,' Frank forced her mind to work, when she really wanted to scream, run through the door, dance, think, sleep, escape from mediaeval nightmares, 'that means that he—or she, the poisoner—wanted one of three things. To kill both Most and me. Or just me, and it was too bad that Most must go as well. Or just Most, and my death would be an unfortunate ancillary circumstance.'

'Precisely.' Sir Barry Stone again pronounced the word according to its meaning, like a well-finned arrow homing towards a target. 'Except that it didn't happen. Only one person died, not two. And there was only one person who could have ensured that result.'

'What?' The temptation to cry out loud became stronger. But it was resisted. After all, Frank had often thought, if you're a woman, and black, and you've succeeded (as she had) in a profession that the whole world regards as the inherent exclusive prerogative of men, white men—large hard tough white men at that—well, you should be able to deal with little things like being accused of murder by the Head of the Kavendish Laboratory. No, not accused. She saw the look in Stone's eye. Just warned.

'You mean that I—I'm the prime suspect. I'm the only one who could have ensured that Most died and I didn't?' Stone nodded.

Enough of sang froid. 'Look,' Frank's voice was slightly raised, tinged with anger. 'I didn't drink from that gold vase because I'd had enough alcoholic poison already.' She stopped—oh, what the hell! 'I mean, I'd had enough booze already. And anyway when we started up again I forgot I hadn't taken a drink.' She remembered the policeman's rule of thumb—if someone gives two excuses, it's likely that neither is true. 'Or both. Oh, what the hell.'

Frank buried her head between two tapering just-brown hands. Barry Stone placed a hand on her shoulder. Not avuncularly. The hand of a friend. 'Look, Frank—and you call me Barry—I'm just letting you see it as an outsider might. I have no doubt in my own mind that it must have been one of the Fellows. Neither James Thorpe nor you had any motive. After all you didn't know about—I mean, you didn't know anyone there, did you?'

'No,' Frank agreed. But I did know of the existence of Project Pasar, if that's what you stopped yourself saying. And Dr Most knew I knew. Is this murder connected with an invention that can perhaps lead to speedy interstellar travel, cheap domestic power, and be the undoubted basis of weapons beyond the power of imagination?

Well, it did now seem like a rather challenging job. A bit

different from unmasking rake-offs that municipal officers were collecting for being a bit selective in the building contracts they awarded. Frank mused on the contrast between this and her last assignment.

'Anyway,' Sir Barry announced with a finality that closed the matter, 'the police will be interviewing all guests at the Feast. And all waiters. They want to see you—' he consulted a piece of folded yellow paper from his shirt pocket, '—at 11.45, in the Master's Study.' Frank wrote it down with a twenty-cent ballpen at the top of a cheap spiral notepad she had just taken from her bag in anticipation of really getting down to work.

'And now,' Sir Barry buttered a piece of toast, thickly, 'we were to talk about your project. Interpersonal relations, in the Kavendish, Lord Johns said. Should be interesting. I expect you'll be able to tell me a thing or two.'

The marmaladed slab was conveyed to the professorial mouth and slowly chewed. Frank was clearly expected to—take the floor? Phew, she should have thought this cover story through a bit more fully. On the other hand, when had there been the time since lunchtime yesterday? Well, fall back on the old family forte—improvise!

She became very serious. Placed her knees together. 'The hypothesis is,' Frank began, trying to invoke the right sort of jargon, 'that people interact differently in places of high achievement, where there is some important work going on, compared to how they would in more mundane circumstances.'

'Don't believe it at all.' Sir Barry again at his most straightforward. 'It wouldn't make a ha'porth of difference. They'd fight, and be jealous, and co-operate, and sulk, and have love affairs, and help and hinder each other just the same, if they were making soap flakes or developing . . .'

Frank opened her mouth as if to say, 'Pasars'.

'Some new form of energy,' Stone concluded.

'Don't you think the pressure . . . ?' Frank began again.

'Balls. The pressure might make things happen a bit faster. But the same things would happen. There's no essential difference, I'm sure of that. Even spying.' Frank's eyebrows shot up, at least mentally. 'It's the same principle there. A rival manufacturer trying to find out your secret whiter-than-white ingredient. Or a foreign country wanting to share in a scientific discovery. There's no real difference. People can still be bought and manipulated. There are some that are honest and others that are crooked, in any line of business.'

Frank had tried one half-slice of toast with a scraping of butter and hardly any marmalade. The second one she plastered. It did taste much better, give Sir Barry his due.

'You know, Frank,' he continued, 'I think there's more to you than that. I don't mean to doubt that you're a sociologist . . .'

Well thanks, Frank almost murmured aloud. After all I am still registered for a PhD in Sociology at Chicago. And I am still interested in—she intoned the dissertation topic, 'Patterns of church-going among contemporary urban populations, and correlation with socio-economic status'. But—she further admitted to herself—not so interested as I am in finding out who killed Dr Most and whether there's a Chinese connection.

'. . . but I suspect you've got some hidden motive. Something else. Lord Johns doesn't mess about and his backing you for a project like that seems to me to be distinctly fishy, fair dinkum it does.'

Frank had, in fact, already decided that she would let Sir Barry in on the nature of her mission. The only argument against was that he must of course be a suspect. But she knew from experience that if the villain knew he was being observed it could be rather more interesting than if he didn't. (And more dangerous, that went without saying.)

It didn't yet seem the right moment, though. Best to raise maximum mileage out of any personal disclosure, get as much as possible in return. Just delay a little while.

'Who'll be the next Master, Barry? I suppose you must be a strong candidate.'

'Was last time. The favourite, they said.' All compassion was now gone out of Stone's voice. Oh my Lord, thought Frank, not very acute am I—for a sociologist.

'Delaney's the one. That's what all the gossip says.'

Gossip? The Master had been murdered close to midnight and there was already a favourite to replace him! Frank's blank look led Sir Barry to explain, somewhat testily: 'In the combination room this morning. Most people eat breakfast there. Oh, we don't waste time here, you know. The election must be held within seven days, by statute, and there'll be a lot of lobbying going on. My word! Pretty exciting time, all in all.'

The King is dead, long live the King, thought Frank. What she said was: 'Do you think Dr Most will be missed? I mean, was he popular? Did the other Fellows like him?' Important to find out why the Master had been murdered. Did someone want his job? Or did they covet Bernice? Or did Most perhaps know too much about Project Pasar?

A servant—gyp, Frank fancied she'd heard them called—entered the room and removed breakfast things, bringing with him a fresh jug of steaming coffee. Sir Barry spoke as if the man didn't exist, or were deaf and dumb.

'He made sure he was popular, did Patrick. Knew so much about all of us that you had to like him, couldn't afford not to. But, funny thing, we all did anyway. He had the sort of qualities one looks for in an administrator. Totally discreet. Didn't interfere, let everyone get on with their own thing. And he did have a few good ideas.' Sir Barry put one hand on Frank's knee and then removed it quickly before providing a summary of the aforegiven encomium, scientific-presentation-fashion: 'Useful fellow, Patrick.'

Might be a lead here. 'What sort of ideas?'

Sir Barry settled back, started filling a meershaum pipe. 'Funny you should ask. I was just going over what to say in my funeral oration for old Pat. Spelling reform, that was his great mission. Make it gradual, he said, about one change every decade. First thing was get rid of *c*. If it's pronounced like *k* then write *k*. *Krimson* and *kake* and all that. Then in words like *sinch* and *synthia* you use *s*. Good idea, one letter less.'

Actually he wasn't the first to suggest that, you know. Not by several thousand. But Frank let Stone continue. She was enjoying watching him talk. Somehow the way he used his hands, circling, gently stabbing home a point—it was all rather hypnotic.

'And then.' Pipe actually to mouth. A quick suck, taken away again. 'In about ten years we'd replace *ch* by *c*, Pat said. One sound, one letter—good principle. So *church* would be *c-u-r-c*. And the College name would be changed of course—no more *h* in Michaelhouse. It's up to us to set an example, the Master was quite right there. Even though it would require an Act of Parliament, of course.'

Of course, sympathised Frank. And, one change every ten years! Just like the English. That was how they dealt with decimalisation. Very gradual shift. First of all stop teaching imperial measures in school—no more converting inches to yards, yards to miles, pints to gallons. But then they deferred actually *making* the change to metres and kilos and litres and Celsius. So one whole generation was growing up not being able to work anything out. . . .

But, for heaven's sake let's get back at least to the subplot. Frank made a determined effort. 'I wouldn't have thought the Mastership would be a very attractive job. Does anyone actually *want* it?'

Sir Barry again took pipe from mouth. It was now stuffed with a certain quantity of tobacco, but unlit. He gazed at Frank as if she had suggested pigs could fly—or that Cambridge were not the finest university on earth. Not horror. Just surprise at such naïvety.

'Everybody wants the job.' A straightforward antipodean answer.

Pipe was lit and puffed as Sir Barry explained that Bernice Dodds was already trumpeting her own case. There'd never been a woman head of one of the traditionally male colleges at Oxford or Cambridge. Frank thought that was a very good point and so, probably, did Sir Barry. As an anthropologist she'd be able to understand people. Sure, if ever Frank had seen anything which reminded her of a tribal society it was Michaelhouse College. And she had been—well—er—the Master's . . . 'particular friend'. Sir Barry smiled as he captured an appropriate formula. Conjugal succession?

But a note of grumpiness did intrude. 'Just because Most had plenty of time to lavish on her. Never got married, you know. And no labs to look after.' The Professor didn't appear to be actually disapproving of love-affairs as such, as long as they were kept in their place. His eyes seemed to glint as they moved on to survey the rest of the field.

Leon Ivanovitch would absolutely love to be Master, and seemed to think he had a real chance. Totally impossible, Sir Barry announced. 'He's only been here four years. And he is a Russian.' To Frank the idea of undergraduates being urged to greater effort through Leon's supply of Slavic jokes was rather irresistible.

Simon Jeffrey? 'Too young.' An impatient response as if not another word were to be said on that score. Absent-minded Andrew Delaney had all the right qualities, it seemed. 'Deuced clever, that fellow'—but it was left unclear as to whether that was a desirable quality in a Master, or if this was just an explanation about how Delaney would achieve his ambition.

There were a couple of Fellows who hadn't been at the Feast. Derek Randall, the history don, and Edward Hemmings, who taught some language or other that was unlikely to attract too many students. Kashmiri, Stone thought it was, or perhaps Korean. They didn't seem to be too strongly fancied. 'And of course it could be someone from outside the college.' Sir Barry let out this admission as if the possibility were an entirely theoretical one. Well, Frank reflected, Michaelhouse did have all the characteristics of an endogamous society.

And Sir Barry? No doubt at all that he'd adore to be elected. The final step, on his path from the broken-down sheep farm near Goondiwindi?

'Surely your present job at the Kavendish is much more exciting? And important. Rather than looking after what is after all just a glorified hall of residence.' Two could play at being straightforward, Frank decided.

Sir Barry ignored the taunt. 'Yes, certainly the Kavendish is an interesting job. It has its moments—trying to spend as much money as possible, and all that.'

For perhaps the twelfth time since she'd stepped off the Delta jet at Gatwick Frank felt lost. In another world, one that had no point of contact with her own. 'You don't try to *overspend.* I mean can you—is it allowed?'

'Oh yes one can. And should.' Sir Barry hunched up elbows on knees, hands clasped in front. 'Not in one's personal life of course. If you or I overspend we'll be declared bankrupt and finish up in jail. The same goes for a business. But what most people don't realise is that completely different principles apply for institutions, and governments, and that sort of thing.'

'Think of it,' he went on. 'Britain always has a trade loss. Every month we buy more than we sell. Big deficit. And the country has a huge National Debt that'll never be paid off. What happens to us? Nothing!' The stem of Sir Barry's pipe was jabbed triumphantly at Frank's sternum. 'Do other countries refuse to trade with us? They can't, their industry would have a terrible recession. It makes no difference at all to a country whether the books are balanced or if they're in total disarray.'

'Yes, but a laboratory,' Frank remonstrated, 'you must have a certain budget.'

'Ah, we do, we do,' Stone agreed, 'and it's very important we spend it. If we don't they'll give us less next year. But if we overspend? Well, the worst is that it comes off next year's budget in advance. That's never happened yet. No, they just give us more this year—and even more next. You see, they expect the Kavendish to overspend. The more you spend the more important you are. It's as simple as that.'

This line of economic thinking Frank found quite novel. Not at all what *her* economics professors had said. Yet it had an air of plausibility. And Sir Barry was reckoned very good and successful at his job. Why then was he suddenly looking sad, almost haggard?

'Our new breakthrough,' he said by way of explanation, 'is extremely cheap. Complex theory, wonderful results. But it costs almost nothing. I can tell you Frank—' Sir Barry's hand again rested lightly, momentarily, on his visitor's knee, '—it really is a source of great worry to me.'

'And the Mastership would be a way out?'

'No, no, it'd be an entirely different ball-game.' He smiled at producing an American idiom for Frank's benefit. 'There you'd have to balance the books, of course.' A far-away look came into Sir Barry's eyes and his voice now sounded distant. 'The Master does have a very nice house, you know, with a private garden to the Cam.'

This is *the* most ridiculous thing, decided Frank. A grown man, an internationally-renowned scientist, wanting to swop Project Pasar for a garden!

'These rooms seem pretty good to me.' Try to jolly him out of such an unseemly mood.

'Indeed they are,' exclaimed Sir Barry, as if it had been someone quite different talking a moment before. 'Would you care to see around my suite? Fifteenth-century, you know. Low doorways, that's the only disadvantage I can see.'

Frank had already got up, and allowed herself to be escorted—first through the doorway—into a study. Shelf upon shelf of leather-bound books right around the room. Yet there was no hint of mustiness. Painstakingly polished wood. Leather-top desk. Brown, everything brown. Frank yearned to set eyes on something bright. A yellow curtain, just a hint of blue sky.

'Hey,' she admired, 'have you read all of these books?'

'Oh no, none of them,' Sir Barry replied complacently. 'They belong to the college you see. Mostly sermons from the seventeenth century. Sort-of like wallpaper. I do read a lot, though—get all the recent novels from the town library in Lion Yard.'

Frank found it galling always being one step behind. 'You do buy some books though, surely? On physics, I mean. Oh, I suppose those are kept in your office at the lab.'

'No, no, no.' Stone seemed to be enjoying his deflation of Frank's ideas about top scientists. 'Haven't bought one for years. Well,' he admitted, 'publishers often do send me them free. But those mostly find their way into the Kavendish library.'

Suppose she were the victim of some gigantic hoax. There was no such thing as Project Pasar. Sampson Ndagbera never wrote any fortuitous formula. Professor Sir Barry Stone couldn't tell a rheostat from a voltmeter. It all seemed to Frank much more likely than the tale Lord Johns had spun. Prime Ministers' husbands and interstellar travel indeed!

Opening the door for Frank to pass into the next room Sir Barry had a flash of remembrance. 'I do subscribe to one journal, you know. *Physics Abstracts*. Helps me keep up with what the other blokes are thinking about.' I wish you wouldn't keep making it worse, Frank wanted to scream, as he added a coda: 'Don't have the time to read it right through though, you know.'

The bedroom. Well, pleasant surprise. Flowery blue wall-paper. Pink-shaded light next to the bed. The bed! Nice to be able to see, with one's own eyes, something known mainly from whisky ads in the *New Yorker*. A large English four-poster. The real thing. And if one said Edwardian it could only be Edward III. Or IV, maybe. Elaborately carved pine pillars, and pink chintzy curtains, pulled right around save on the side facing Frank and Sir Barry.

'Hardly ever sleep in College, of course. But it's good to have it here to fall back on.' Frank looked at Sir Barry—no, he hadn't intended it as a pun.

'How about trying it out now, then?'

Sir Barry looked, quickly, at Frank. Found her gazing out of the window, across the Cam at the clock turret in St John's, on top of which some lively undergraduates had hung a chamber-pot. Yes, she had said it. Indeed why not. His mind was trying to think fast enough to deal with a situation which, while not unique in his experience, certainly hadn't happened in the last twenty years. Why bother to think? Quite the wrong course of action. Actions, not words, Barry, his mother had scolded the reflectant schoolboy, in that adobe Queensland farmhouse.

'Well, why not,' Sir Barry heard himself respond. Better not say any of the other things that occurred to him, like just having time before she had to go and see the police. No, not at all appropriate.

But what to do next? Sir Barry's indecision was resolved by

Frank le Roux, Her Majesty's chosen investigator, turning round with a soft smile, a melting look, turning around to be kissed. To be grasped by Barry Stone. Hugged firmly, delicately, just enough. Frank's heavy-knit rust sweater, for cold May days in Cambridge. Biscuit-coloured tee-shirt. No bra. Never any bra. Jeans. Sandals. Men's clothes always take a little longer to discard. Not too much longer.

Barry Stone, Fellow of the Royal Society, Knight Bachelor, éminence grise, Director of the Kavendish Laboratory, unsuccessful candidate for the Mastership of Michaelhouse College. Not given to post-breakfast encounters on his ancient four-poster bed. Not averse to them. Moving gently, easily. His wife, why think about one's wife? Who knew what she got up to? Nothing, probably. It was the first time that Barry had . . . since, that Colloquium in Amsterdam. Eight years ago—could it be? Thought evaporated into sensation, rhythmic, engulfing, climbing, falling, reaching out, filling every crack and cavity and crevice. Warmth of bodies. Warmth of joy, of achieving, reaching. Gruff, half-swallowed professorial grunts of pleasure as Frank herself seemed easily, lightly, to peak. A deep, contented moan of ecstasy, like a long-held trumpet note.

Now—she'd meant to earlier—Frank put out one hand to draw across the last pink curtain. Totally enclosed. Like camping in the Appalachians. Or anywhere? Gentle stroking.

'I have a confession to make.' Surely the time would never be more ripe.

'Yes, Frankie?'

'You were right, Barry. I'm not a sociologist.' Correction. 'Not just a sociologist. You may not believe this but I'm a private investigator.'

Quite frankly I'd be prepared to believe any damn thing right now, Barry mused. No need to say anything.

'Lord Johns told me about Project Pasar.' She felt his body stiffen, almost imperceptibly. Then relax again. 'He's worried about the secret being stolen. Thinks it is being, bit by bit. By the Chinese. I'm supposed to find out how, and stop it.' Then, sensing in the movement of Stone's shoulder—whether or not it was intended—a question. 'I suppose because I'm the most unlikely detective. No one *ought to*—' Frank stressed the words as if, were they to, it would be Barry Stone's fault, '—no one ought to guess what I'm up to. And,' surely room for a modicum of self-sell, 'I do have a fair record of success in things like this.'

When Sir Barry spoke it was with an altogether different air. The slightly-bumbly donnish façade had given way to an intense businesslike tone. He continued to run his hands gently through Frank's hair—there was no contradiction in that.

'All right. I'm surprised but if that's what HMG wants it's okay with me. Was I to be told, by the way?'

'Well.' There seemed to Frank no possibility of subterfuge. 'No. I don't think so. Patrick Most knew who I was. That was all, I think.'

Sir Barry Stone's sigh escaped past Frank's left ear. 'Yes, he knew, goodness knows how. He knew everything. But I honestly do think—with that one exception—it is a well-kept secret. Sampson and Leon and I, we are the team. Any one of us could reconstruct the whole thing, given about a year and a computer. Andrew Delaney had checked some of the equations. But he doesn't know the complete story. Doesn't know how breath-taking the final result is. Doesn't seem interested—he's just that sort of chap.'

'What about everyone else in the Kavendish?' Frank tried to see Stone's watch, which had not been discarded. Wouldn't do to be late for the police. And have the gyp come searching for her!

'No. They all work in different teams, on their own projects.' Now it was possible to believe that Barry Stone was responsible for the greatest scientific breakthrough since—since the wheel? He acted, thought, plainly spoke like Frank's idea of a scientist. And added one slightly hesitant rider. 'Except for Louise?'

'Louise Bates?' The brassy debater from New Hampshire.

'That's right. She is good, you know, when she bothers to apply herself. Louise was working with Leon on one line that just happened to tie in with Equation Eight. It was a total surprise. Otherwise of course she wouldn't have been let near it. I mean even then, last October, we had a fair idea what it might all lead to. And I think—' Stone paused to scratch his right thigh and did the same to Frank for good measure. 'I suspect she has some idea of what's happening. Cute cookie, little Louise.'

Just time for one more sounding. 'How reliable are they, Barry? Sampson and Leon? Lord Johns said that Sampson got the critical equation by luck or something. Surely that would be easy to steal?'

Professorial hands fell idle. But he kissed Frank full on the mouth before replying. Firmly, no lingering. 'Not quite. It was a whole series of equations. About—oh, more than a hundred. They all tie together. But you couldn't exactly infer one from the others. Not unless you had Ndagbera's intuitive genius, that is.'

He drew back the nearest curtain, the one opposite the window. One beam of sunlight blossomed through a tiny crack in the clouds, fell squarely on Frank's face. Pert mouth, high cheekbones, hair lying across ear and neck and breast.

'There are precisely two hundred and fifteen pages setting out the basic theory of Pasars. Fifty-three of them are in a safe in my office at the lab, the combination known only to me. No one else. If I die it would have to be blown open. They have been seen by only Leon and Sampson. The other pages are treated with care but not locked away.'

Stone gestured towards an envelope on the low marble table between bed and window. Phew, reflected Frank, at least you might put them under the mattress.

'And Leon?' she asked.

'Ndagbera and Ivanovitch are both totally above suspicion. Hell, Leon left Moscow because he couldn't stand communism. Wrote to the American papers to tell them so. And then he *had* to leave.' Which is not exactly the same thing as leaving of one's own accord, Frank reflected as Barry was adding: 'Leon is as reliable as—as—well, as me.'

No harm in asking the sixty-four thousand dollar one, Frank decided, as her finger traced the line of Stone's backbone. 'Who would be selling the Pasar Principle to the Chinese, then, Barry?'

'Well, I'd assumed it was Pat Most.' A tone of professorial

surprise, as if to a freshman who had forgotten Newton's Second Law.

'But why?' Frank persisted.

'Search me. Maybe they offered him a case of antique Chinese brandy or something.' Which seemed to put an end to that line of questioning.

Stone began to outline the application of Pasars as he got up and dressed. This accorded exactly with Lord Johns' summary. It sounded too good to be true. As if everything had suddenly been multiplied by a million, power-wise, and divided by the same figure, cost-wise. Only more than that. Faster-than-light drive? An impossibility realised.

Then Stone began to explain some of the physics, which Frank found from the first word totally incomprehensible. Oh for a mini-recorder. Although that, she reflected, would probably not be in the best interests of Her Majesty's Government.

'Barry,' she interrupted, as he was trying for the third time to knot a dark green Michaelhouse tie. 'Don't you ever want to escape from all this?' Frank's gesture took in St John's, Trinity, and the ugly square tower of the University Library across the river.

'I mean, Pasars might make a better world. Where you wouldn't have to spend as much money as possible. No playing games. Mankind could have enough food. People would have time to think and dance and sing, and work at meaningful tasks, with pride and satisfaction.' My God, thought Frank, I have gone too far. Sound like Marx. (Or Plato?)

Stone, though, was suddenly enthusiastic. A third side to the professorial personality emerged as he gave Frank a lightning kiss, opened the door to the dining room, coffee jug now cold. 'That's what keeps me going.' His voice had become higher with excitement. 'Pasars are the key to—to a new world. Only—' the lugubrious mantle of Senior Fellow descended once more, '—how are we to achieve it? Russia and America would just blow each other to smithereens if they got the Pasar Principle. And Britain . . . ?' He shrugged his shoulders and, as if on cue, a new, blacker cloud covered the sun.

'Well, thanks for breakfast, Barry.' Frank tried to sound brighter than she felt. 'And now for the police. Sure hope they can find out who poisoned the Master.'

'If they can't solve a crime here, they'll never solve one.'

'What do you mean?'

'Didn't you know?' Stone replied, poker-faced. 'St Michael is the patron saint of policemen.'

III

As Frank approached the Master's study who should emerge but Dr Leon Ivanovitch, face wreathed in smiles. Surely they hadn't been swopping policeman jokes? Nothing seemed impossible where Leon was concerned.

She was put in a capacious armchair, sinking right down into the soft moquette. Frank would rather have sat upright. But perhaps that was part of Inspector Slocombe's technique. Right under the window, too, so that every facial expression could be clearly noted.

The interrogation—if it could be called that—didn't take long. Although, as the Inspector remarked, this was just a preliminary interview. He considered it likely that a Detective Superintendent might be sent up from 'the Yard'. Dr Most was, after all, a well-known man. If not a particularly important one, Frank added to herself, or a particularly clever one, or even—in all likelihood—a particularly good one.

'I believe you'd be a critical witness, Miss le Roux, since you were 'olding the golden jug when the picture dislodged itself from the wall. Or so I have it from Sir Barry.' This was no Cambridgeshire accent. Frank did a double-take. Oxford, West Country. Easy, slow, relaxed drawl, put anyone at their ease. Drawn-out vowels: 'from the waaall'. Well, she reflected, no reasons why policemen, like dons, shouldn't occasionally shift allegiance.

Then, at Frank's nod. 'Just what did you do after placing the jug on the table? I want you to think very carefully, now.'

'I walked over, away from the serving door, to examine the picture of Josiah Wentworth.'

Inspector Slocombe appeared to record each of her words in longhand. Then he contemplated what had been written, sucking at the end of his pencil. Looked up at Frank, like a kindly but determined schoolmaster. 'And why would you do that?'

Frank felt helpless. Engulfed—drowned—in the Master's deep armchair. 'Well—there seemed to be enough people round the picture that had fallen.'

'I mean—' I mean you haven't answered my question, was what the Inspector's look said, 'I mean why did you choose that moment to look at,' a quick glance at notebook, 'Josiah Wentworth?'

Good question. Why didn't I just sit down where I was? 'Well,' Frank began, truthfully, 'everyone else was up—we had been sitting for a long time you know. And—and I wanted to find out more about Josiah Wentworth.'

'Why?'

'Well,' she refused to get flustered, 'people had been saying that he was a famous man. No, I don't mean that. The whole point was that he wasn't famous. No one had heard of him. He was supposed to be . . .' Frank struggled for some suitable word. Not 'great', Most had admitted that. 'Good.' It all sounded so lame.

'Ah, "good".' Inspector Slocombe pronounced the word as if it had a totally different connotation for the Fellows of Michaelhouse College, and their festive guests, from the simple, direct meaning that 'good' carried for the rest of the populace.

There were some more questions, about how long she'd be staying in town. About her knowledge of poisons. Almost non-existent—they just hadn't figured in the crooked rackets that were Frank's normal line of business. And her reason for being there. The mention of Lord Johns brought instant deference. It really was quite amazing, Frank reflected—the power of a title. Especially within a class-ridden society like England.

It was a relief to escape into the damp, windy quadrangle. Ancient, grey walls of hall and library and student staircases. Hard rock coming out of one open third floor casement. Incongruous. Demonaic carved heads on high stone pillars looked down on the pond, goldfish still visible between lily leaves—the soup last night can't have been too bad after all. Frank looked again at the stone gargoyles. Kings and Archbishops and long-forgotten Masters, solemn-faced vigilant guardians of tradition. The record finished. Silence. Large drops of rain came 'plop, plop, plop' on to rectangular stone slabs that went across the lawn. 'Work, work, work,' they seemed to say to Frank as she shivered, hurried through the great arch into Trinity Street. Left, past the children's bookshop, and down towards Great St Mary's as its clock showed 12.30.

Lord Johns had suggested Frank join him for a counter lunch at the Eagle, an old coaching inn on Bene't Street. After that he must return to London, there was no doubt work waiting at the Home Office. Yes, I'd think there would be, Frank refrained from saying. She tried to imagine a Departmental Head in Washington taking the best part of two days off to attend a Feast. (But who knows, perhaps they do.)

There was his Lordship atop a high stool at the bar, half-way through a pint of Guinness. Round white face, glistening as if it had been freshly polished that morning. And they talk about some kinds of black people having shiny faces, Frank ruminated. 'A glass of cider, please.' Eager mouthful to relieve thirst. Phew, if she'd known it would be that strong tomato juice might have been safer.

'I'm sorry to have dragged you into this mess,' Lord Johns began as if he were talking to a lady, some delicate cousin whom a great-aunt had asked that great care be taken of, instead of to a hired detective for whom sudden murder should be—in fact, was—a fairly unremarkable occurrence.

'But,' he became more businesslike, 'you'll see why I said the late Master would be useful to you. He knew a lot, perhaps more than I realised. And now he's paid the price.' Well at least Lord Johns seemed a trifle saddened by Most's demise, which was more than you could say of Sir Barry Stone and—by his testimony—the other Fellows.

'You think Patrick Most was murdered because of his knowledge of Project Pasar?'

'Certainly something to do with that. Either he knew too much, or he wouldn't pass it on. What else could it be? I don't really think any of the Fellows would poison him to get the Mastership, do you?'

The possibility hadn't occurred to Frank. Murder Most for the crummy old Mastership! Well, Barry Stone had said that everyone wanted it. But why?

'Most murders aren't committed for important reasons,' she replied. 'Sexual jealousy or disappointment is a frequent motive. Or all sorts of petty things that to outsiders wouldn't seem worth raising one's voice over.'

'This is Cambridge,' Lord Johns began and then stopped. As well he might. Frank took another sip of her cider. Murdering someone for the Mastership? This is Cambridge all right—but in which century?

'I must impress upon you that no one should know of your mission.' Lord Johns regarded Frank over the top of his rimless spectacles. 'Especially not the Pasar team—Stone or Ivanovitch or that African, Ndagbera.'

The necessity for reply was avoided by the arrival of two plates bearing what Lord Johns described as Grosvenor Pie. Thick hard pastry around a mixture of chopped veal and ham, with a boiled egg in the middle. Frank cut off a corner. Tasty, but indescribably heavy, especially after a breakfast of kippers and Sir Barry Stone.

Frank le Roux, brought from New Orleans to guard the British Government's colossal secret, their one claim to fame in an era of decaying decadence. Frank le Roux looked to Lord Johns for instructions. A plan of attack. Who should she work with? Where might the leak lie? What to do if she should find it? How to know when she *had* found it? Frank realised she wouldn't recognise a page of the Pasar document. Wouldn't know it from a report on nuclear reactors, or advanced crystallography. Did it have 'Pasars' written on every page?

'We prefer you to operate on your own, my dear. Prime Minister's explicit instructions.' But I bet she didn't say 'my dear'. 'Do whatever you think fit. We do have our own security people on the job of course but it is thought best that you do not—aaah—intersect. Any lead you can get, ring me at this number.' Lord

Johns scribbled seven digits on his paper napkin, which was pushed across to Frank. 'It's unlisted. And you can get me at it twenty-four hours a day.'

But what about now, Frank shook her head in bewilderment, you aren't at it now, are you? This job was either the biggest compliment that had ever been paid her, or else Lord Johns didn't want her to succeed, for some reason of his own. Was he a suspect? This hadn't occurred to Frank before. Well, if he knew of Project Pasar he must, automatically, be one. But he had engaged Frank to catch the spy. On the Prime Minister's instructions—although she only had Lord Johns' word for that. Well, stranger things had been known.

Lord Johns finished one helping of pie and transferred half of Frank's slice to his own plate. Not that she was planning to eat the rest, but it was nice to be left the option. 'That was a fine Feast last night, wasn't it? You really can't beat these old colleges for tradition and style.'

Frank tried to force a grin of approval. 'Who would you fancy for the Mastership, Lord Johns?'

Knife and fork were laid down. Here was a really important question. 'None of the Fellows here, that's clear. Barry Stone, take away his knighthood and, after all, he's just an Australian.'

'Would you . . .' Frank was going to add 'support Andrew Delaney', but after the first two words Lord Johns took over.

'Would I? Yes, certainly I'd consider it. After all, to be elected Master of one's old college is—well, it is the highest honour one could receive.'

Frank's mouth fell open. Barry Stone was right. Only when he'd said that everyone wanted the job, Frank thought he'd meant all the Fellows. It turned out it really was everyone. Everyone in England?

'You'd give up your political career?' Frank had heard tell that if Britain ever did decide once more to put a man into the highest office, then Lord Johns had as good a chance of being Prime Minister as anyone else. But he'd prefer the Mastership of Michaelhouse?

There didn't seem too much more to say. The official Mercedes had been left, quite illegally, outside King's College and it had attracted no ticket despite there being two parking wardens within sight. The House of Lords sticker doing its work. Lord Johns waved gaily as he took off—almost literally—to the south.

Frank walked slowly past the gelato man and into King's. Dowdy buildings on to the road that were inconsequential support for the magnificence of the Chapel. She stood solemnly, to admire its beauty. A hundred years it had been in the building, but King's College Chapel would endure for millennia.

'Beautiful, isn't it. But what a waste!'

Those familiarly arrogant vowels. Frank turned round to discover she had been joined by Andrew Delaney, no less. Fresh-faced, college scarf splayed out over a Fair Isle sweater, looking for all the world like a student.

'What do you mean? Why is it a waste?'

'I should have thought it was obvious,' the Professor of Pure Mathematics continued. 'In the fifteenth century religion was *the* guiding force in the world. And we must certainly be grateful that it provided gems of this order. But that's all in the past. Did you know that King's has more active Marxists among its Fellows than any other college? And yet they still hold religious services here! Tst, tst.' The clicks of disapprobation were accompanied by a sadly shaken head.

Frank was still having difficulty keeping up. 'What would you do with it then, Andrew?' She hadn't realised—hadn't been told—that he was a Marxist. And surely it was rather relevant information. 'Use it for readings of the Communist Manifesto? Set to music, perhaps?'

'Heaven forbid.' Delaney showed a hint of amusement, slightly more than would be demanded by politeness. 'No, just keep it for concerts and suchlike. And use it more as an Art Gallery. Keep the name, you know, as a relic of what it used to be. It's part of our history and should be treated as that. No contemporary relevance at all.'

Frank didn't herself actively espouse any religion. But she did have a certain predilection for churches. The building would of course remain. It just wouldn't be used for religious services. And if the men of King's were predominantly atheistic . . .

Still trying to grope towards a logical solution, Frank's attention was suddenly caught by a neat crocodile of small boys coming across King's Bridge towards the Chapel. Only they were all dressed in smart black suits, like miniature versions of the head waiter on Michaelhouse High Table. And top hats. Twelve years old, no more, and each had on his head a little shiny top hat.

'Andrew?' A touch on the arm.

The languorous professorial gaze followed Frank's outstretched finger. Another sad shake of the head. 'See what I mean? The choir, poor little buggers. How those Fellows can countenance such a charade beats me. Never a thought about moving with the times.'

They began walking back towards the street. 'Not that we don't have room for change at Michaelhouse.' Did Frank detect a wistful note, an overtone of 'and they'll get it when I become Master'? This Mastership was plainly an important game, likely almost to outpulse Pasars.

'What changes, Andrew?'

Delaney's face suddenly took on a vague look—or should one term it abstract? 'Oh, lots of things. Look, do call me Andy. And can I show you round Cambridge a bit?'

'I'd like nothing better, Andy.'

'Can I call you Frankie?'

'Please don't. That's reserved for people who I know particularly well. Let's just stick to "Frank" for now.'

'Alright then.' Delaney assented with slight disappointment—and a considerable measure of ambition—as he steered his sightseeing party of one past St Catherine's College, 'rather dull, nothing to look at there', down into Queens'.

The mathematical bridge, a wooden structure across the Cam that was held in position by sheer theory, it seemed. Not a nut or bolt or nail. Just pieces of wood at the correct angles, all strains and stresses calculated to a nicety. And it felt solid enough underfoot, as Professor Delaney shouted across to a drab-looking girl in a headscarf on Silver Street Bridge, next one down. 'Hello there, Deirdre, how's the old head-hunter treating you?'

'Just someone from my Encounter Group,' he explained to Frank, 'secretary who has trouble with her boss. Sorry, shouldn't say that. It's all supposed to stay within the Group, you see.'

'What are you working on now, Andrew? Andy, I mean.' Frank wished she'd taken a few more Math courses back at Harvard. How to know what might be related to Pasars and what couldn't be?

'I am having another go at Fermat's Last Theorem. You know it?'

Frank didn't. She'd never felt more ignorant about almost everything.

But Delaney was up to providing a lightning résumé. 'French mathematician. Seventeenth-century. Brilliant number theorist. Proved all sorts of important theorems. But this one he didn't prove. Scribbled that he had a proof in the margin of a volume of Diophantes.' They passed what looked like a church but was in fact the old building of Cambridge University Press. That *is* a church across the road, St Botolph's.

'Funny thing is that no one's ever been able to prove it. Although we don't doubt that it is true.'

Maybe that was what Sampson Ndagbera had done? Well, any straw is better than none when you're groping in the dark. 'Is it hard to explain the theorem, Andy?'

'No easier thing in the world. You know there are lots of numbers a, b, c such that $a^2 = b^2 + c^2$. Like $5^2 = 4^2 + 3^2$ and $13^2 = 12^2 + 5^2$ and all that?'

Hurrah! This was the first thing since she arrived in England which Frank had been expected to know and did know. 'Yes, I remember, right-angled triangles and Pythagoras' theorem.'

A congratulatory professorial hand slapped Frank on the back. Almost knocked her to the ground as they turned into Corpus Christi College. Delaney's own from when he was an undergraduate, it appeared. 'Well, Fermat said that there were no numbers a, b and c such that $a^n = b^n + c^n$ where n is three or more. And there aren't. We've had the computer check up well into the millions and old Fermat was right. The only thing is that no one's yet been able to *prove* the damn thing.'

Well, Frank reflected, as they looked up at Delaney's old room in the Old Court, circa 1360, if Fermat's Last Theorem has long been known then it can hardly be a significant factor in Pasar theory.

Down Free School Lane. 'This is where they split the atom.' Frank's attention was now total. 'In the old Cavendish. With a C. Before Barry Stone condescended to follow Most's little foibles and spell it with a K. And then they moved the whole caboosh out of town, along the Madingley Road. You ought to see round it some time.'

'Yes,' Frank agreed, 'I'm going over there tomorrow morning. Sir Barry kindly offered to provide an office. I hope to study interpersonal attitudes within the lab situation.' Frank had almost forgotten about her cover. And certainly Delaney paid no attention at all.

'Emmanuel College next,' he promised, 'special stop for important American tourists. That's where a lot of the Pilgrim Fathers came from. Including your John Harvard, I'm told.'

Suddenly a figure appeared, almost jumped, out of the Anthropology Museum, veering off at the last minute to avoid impact with Frank. A neat, attractive figure. Seemed distraught. Became downright angry at the sight of Frank and Andrew Delaney.

'You still here?' Dr Bernice Dodds directed an instinctive remark at Frank. Then she immediately recovered herself, smiled, and held out a hand to be shaken. 'I'm sorry. You can understand we're all a bit on edge after the Master's death.' Why don't you say 'murder', Frank wanted to ask. Most is dead but he didn't die—he was killed, poisoned, got out of the way.

Frank stammered a few disjointed sentences about her study taking a few weeks perhaps. 'We must have a talk.' Bernice was now all sweetness. 'After all, the only difference is that you sociologists study people who wear western clothes while we anthropologists go after the rest of the world—those who wear sarongs or raffia skirts or just go naked. And I *do* know a bit about how people interact around here.'

A wave to Delaney and Bernice was gone. They turned and watched her progress back in the direction of Michaelhouse. Walking fast, but with poise and style. It is nice that once in a while expectations are fulfilled. The author of *Primitive Procreation* turned out exactly as she should. Sexy, charming, full of life and hard as nails.

And, thought Frank, as she only half-listened to the next section of Delaney's tour, just how much did Bernice know? If Most was on to Project Pasar—wouldn't he have shared at least something of it with his de facto spouse? Dr Dodds had been to China recently—Frank remembered a TV interview and the justification for including sinolist proclivities in the book, third edition. It wasn't as if China could be described as a primitive nation? But perhaps their sexual positions were? Frank couldn't remember the rationale Bernice had offered.

Into the centre of town. Market Hill. 'But there isn't a hill? There are no hills at all. Cambridge must be the flattest place in the world,' Frank protested.

Delaney muttered something about different etymology, and then excused himself for a moment. Frank idly looked through a stack of records while watching, out of the corner of an eye, Delaney in earnest conversation with a freckle-faced youth selling apples at the next wooden market stall. Some good blues reissues—Blind Willie McTell, Charley Patton.

'Sorry about that. Roger. He's another member of the Group. Used to be a student here, local lad. Had to drop out. Family troubles, you know.'

Well, thought Frank, when the revolution comes, Professor Delaney, there may be no more Chairs of Math. But you could probably get employment as a social worker. Or headline writer—nice, taut summaries.

They walked up the narrow cobbles of Rose Crescent. Health Food Shop, elderly assistants climbing narrow ladders to fetch glass jars of dried apricots from a top shelf.

At about this stage in a job Frank expected things to begin

falling into place. A pattern should emerge. Of allegiances and jealousies and intrigues—which somehow made a coherent whole, in terms of which the crime could be examined, dissected, motives analysed. Future moves predicted, foreshadowed, prevented.

But here, in Cambridge, there were dozens of disparate bits of information. Just that. Like a jigsaw puzzle none of whose pieces fitted together.

Andrew Delaney. Mathematician. Marxist. Prime candidate for the Mastership of Michaelhouse College—although Frank inferred that he wouldn't be interested in talking on that topic. Sallow Cambridge aesthete, accent rather right of the Queen. Jolly encounters with spotty secretary and unsure apple seller. Supervisor of Sampson Ndagbera. . . .

'Tell me about your student, Mr Ndagbera. He is your student, isn't he?'

Delaney was negotiating a left-turn back to what must be one of the smallest churches ever. 'Certainly, he's my student in the eyes of the Faculty. But, in truth, I have never met anyone less in need of a teacher. Sampson is the most original, intuitive mathematician since—since Ramujan.' But the tour was not yet finished: 'What do you think of our college chapel, Frank?'

They had stopped in front of St Michael's Church. 'We share it with the townspeople, of course,' he added. 'Have done for five hundred years.'

'Pity it's got to stop,' Frank commented drily.

'What do you mean?'

'Well, when you become Master I suppose religious services will cease.' Frank poked her head inside. 'Reminds me a bit of Preservation Hall. Same size and shape. Be terrific for a jazz club, you know.'

'Hey, I say!'

It was nice to score a point, for a change. Frank was enjoying Delaney's discomfort. The struggle between Marxist logic, a mathematicians's yen for consistency, and the all-hallowed traditions of one's own college.

'We couldn't do that, you know. I mean it wouldn't be fair to the townspeople.' Ah, the old opiate for the masses, Frank intoned to herself. 'Anyway,' Delaney concluded, 'this is much older than King's Chapel, you know.'

Hard to keep on one topic. But worth another try. 'How is Sampson getting on with his thesis, Andy?'

'Finished it in three months. Fifteen pages, that's all. Sheer quality. But of course he won't submit it for another year. Wants the full term of his scholarship, you see. I don't see him much now, works mostly at the Kavendish with that obscene Russian on some new-fangled sort of field theory. You know, the thing Einstein was always trying to crack.'

It would be nice to find out what sort of man this Ndagbera was. But the guided tour was not yet complete.

'This,' Delaney waved the end of his scarf towards the left side of Trinity Street, 'I'm sure that this is the shop where Bertrand Russell used to buy his tobacco.'

Heavens preserve us, as Frank's mother was wont to remark! Who cares? And did Newton scuff his shoe on that cobble? They were now on home territory, and passed through the small open aperture in the great wooden gate of Michaelhouse. Into that austere, solemn court. Still silent. Or could one hear the scratchings of quill pens as nervous students prepared for Tripos examinations?

Delaney had stopped. 'You know the story. One day he suddenly threw his tin of tobacco in the air and said—' Delaney tossed his scarf end high and assumed what he imagined was an imitation of Russell's shrill strained voice. 'He cried out: "Great God in boots, the ontological argument is sound." I ask you, whoever heard of—'

Bored quite to *her* boots Frank had momentarily looked up at the stone gargoyles. An intuitive, fortunate glance.

'Look out!' She suddenly, like a whipcrack, pushed Andrew Delaney away so that he fell heavily on the flagstones three yards off, scarf over face. Frank herself sprang in the opposite direction. Jumped out, her own landfall muffled, covered over a thousandfold by the impact of a tremendous block of stone which completely filled the space between professor and investigator.

Crash! The whole court rocked as the thirty-foot fall of an ancient face, carved in hard stone, dug into the pathway. Paving slabs buckled, pieces of gargoyle sprayed out, bouncing across the grass, just missing Frank le Roux and her kindly afternoon guide. Second near escape from death in—in sixteen hours, Frank rued, as she spied one corner of her red-shoulder-bag peeping from under the metre-square block. Dislodged by her leap into safety, the bag itself was now lying in the spot where Delaney and Frank had stood. It was squarely under that monstrous stone face. Flat. Squashed very flat.

IV

Shocks take a while to register. How long varies with the person and the occasion—a few minutes, an hour or two, days, sometimes years. Frank picked herself up, could just see Delaney over the solid block of stone that would have squashed either of them to a pancake—not even recognisable dental work by which the remains could have been identified.

Heads appeared out of windows around the court. So there were people there, many people, working amid that now-forgotten silence. Heads disappeared. Two, three dozen pairs of feet running down wooden staircases into the court. To see if they could help, to survey the damage, to lament the loss of a fine gargoyle, applaud the miraculous escape from death of Delaney, known quantity, and of Frank le Roux, blond almond-skinned visitor from across the Atlantic.

The porter was busy organising, fussing over Delaney, every other word a 'sir'. Frank simply slipped away. Back into the street. Bought a postcard, to send to her mother, from the small shop-plus-post-office next to Heffer's big bookstore. No views of Michaelhouse available, what a shame. Imposing picture of Trinity Great Court. Frank crossed the road and went into Trinity, hoping that such attention to a rich rival would not be taken amiss at Michaelhouse.

Sitting in the middle of that vast quadrangle, under the fountain. Just now New Orleans seemed like such a familiar, *safe* place. The weather, Frank informed her mother, was lousy, but people interesting and food good. 'Went to a Feast last night.' It's funny how words can take on new meanings. Until yesterday 'feast' would have conjured up schoolgirls gorging on cream cakes at midnight, from some Victorian novel. But now it seemed a perfectly normal description for adult men and women solemnly being served elaborate recipes on a high stage overlooking a dark empty hall. With music—of course.

Then, time lapse of half an hour, the shock started to act. Frank's hand began to shake, needed an effort to control as she signed the card. Mother would be pleased that Frank was exposed to 'all that history'. If she only knew to what she was being exposed!

The poisoned chalice could have killed one or both of two people. Dr Patrick Most, victim claimed. And Frank le Roux, who had escaped just because she had forgotten to drink of the toast, although it was the high spot of Mr Ffothergill-Hawthorn-Williams' bequest banquet.

The falling gargoyle could have killed one or both of two people. Professor Andrew Delaney and the same Frank le Roux, who had just chanced to look up at the most fortuitous moment. Had she heard some noise—the stone face beginning to separate itself from the building? Or someone levering it off?

Most had been Master. Delaney was favourite to succeed him. Had that been the motive? Was some power-hungry Fellow crazy enough to kill, twice, to achieve high office?

Most knew of Project Pasar and so did Delaney, at least in part. Was that the motive? Were they refusing to supply information? Or had they done so and were now dispensable, best got out of the way, evidence removed?

Or was the gargoyle incident pure accident, unconnected with Most's murder?

There was one further alternative, which Frank forced herself to face as she walked slowly back into Michaelhouse court, the stone slab now lying in its corner unattended, unremarked. Silence once more reigned, but it seemed now to be not peaceful—rather grim, eerie, a silence full of foreboding.

Across towards the combination room for afternoon tea, indulgent English habit. What if the target had been somewhat different. Not Most or Delaney but the one person common to both incidents. What if the aim were to kill Frank le Roux. Why? Because she was in Cambridge to stop the leak? But no one knew save Most, and he was the one who had died.

'*There* you are. We wondered what had happened to you,' Simon Jeffrey's warm Yorkshire concern as he placed a hand across Frank's shoulder and handed her some tea. Bone China cup containing Assam tea, deep clear colour which it seemed a shame to sully by the addition of milk. 'You were very nifty. Saved your life and that of our friend Andrew, here.'

He gestured towards an armchair where Delaney sat, rather more hunched than usual, both hands clasped around a huge brandy bulb. Shivering with delayed fright.

'The perils of history.' It was somehow comforting to hear the thick Russian accent of Leon Ivanovitch. 'And let me tell you, there is no way out. Even after revolution the buildings remain. Change the social system but history can always fall on your head.'

'Yes, but the point surely is—was it pushed?' Bernice Dodds was there too, out to temper Ivanovitch's levity. 'That gargoyle of John Fisher was right outside the window at the top landing of staircase E. Someone could have reached out with a metal rod and just wobbled it a bit. We knew it wasn't all that safe. I've been telling the Master for years, and the previous one, that he couldn't rely on the power of heaven to keep John Fisher on high.'

'True, that was what first occurred to me.' Ivanovitch, the efficient scientist, following up every avenue of inquiry. Hey, you'd make a good detective, Frank stored up to tell him some time. 'I went up E and examined the moorings—is that how you say? There were no tell-tale marks of levering. The stone beneath had crumbled, that is all. No foul play suspected.'

Frank finally found words. 'What do the police say?'

'Ee, there'll be no need to be calling the police in,' Simon Jeffrey reassured her. 'Bit of stone falling. Lamentable happening but couldn't be avoided. Senior Fellow's been informed. Barry says he can't get away from Kavendish just now but he's against calling in the police. Enough trouble already with that poisoning last night.'

Was it only last night? It seemed to Frank that she'd been in Cambridge for most of her life.

'Should be given wide publicity, though.' Andrew Delaney spoke from his chair in a hoarse, breathless creak. 'Use it to get those rich buggers—' he was apparently referring to Michaelhouse alumnii who had prospered in the world of business and commerce, '—to give a bit more to our building appeal. Needn't have happened if all those columns had been done up. Poor John Fisher might still be smiling down on us.'

'Oh, I think he can be put back,' Bernice Dodds reassured Delaney. Didn't anything ever ruffle her? Did she still retain that satanic chicness when sampling some exotic figure-of-eight position with an indulgent African chief, before assigning it three or four stars in her consumer's guide to bizarre sex? 'Only the nose is seriously damaged and a . . .'

Frank stole away. An hour's sleep. Try to recover a bit of composure before her dinner date with Simon Jeffrey. And then what sounded like a really interesting debate at the Cambridge Union, that conquered bastion over which Louise Bates now presided.

Sleep, walk, eat. Eat with Simon in a Chinese restaurant that seemed peculiarly English-Chinese.

'Never in my life have I eaten more. How is it everyone around here isn't totally bloated?'

Frank's remark received a reply only when Simon Jeffrey felt the need to take breath in between conveying chopstick-loads of Szechuan chicken the short distance from raised bowl to open mouth. 'Yes,' he agreed, 'eating is a pretty important part of life in Cambridge. Eating and drinking and talking, those are the best parts of life, aren't they?'

Frank forbore from adding to the list.

'You see, we all work in different departments or laboratories. And the only way people really get together to form an academic community is over a bit of chow in college.'

But how can you act as an academic community when there's an agreement not to talk of work, or the pictures on the wall (or women?), Frank wondered. She just stated the obvious: 'But we aren't eating in college.'

'Oh no,' above a sigh of relief. Jeffrey certainly did merit admiration for being able to eat and sigh and talk all at the same time. 'One does get a bit fed up with college food, you know.'

From Frank's short experience of the Michaelhouse kitchen this was akin to an Inca King complaining about too much bright reflection from all that gold around the place.

'And exercise,' Simon retracked the conversation, 'is very important here. All those marshy fens can play havoc with one's chest unless one indulges in some very vigorous activity.'

Something odd had been happening. Frank suddenly realised that Simon's Yorkshire accent was gradually evaporating, and he was now speaking in something close to BBC English.

'What exercise do you do, Simon?'

'Oh, climbing over roofs, that sort of thing. Used to do more when I was a student. Lots of interesting spires and towers in Cambridge, really the place is made for it. Scramble up and pop something on top. Very hard stone here—not like Oxford—so it's perfectly safe!

'Have a duck's foot.' Simon helped himself to three as Frank gingerly transferred one of the webbed morsels to her plate. 'Don't do as much of it now as I'd like.' Then he added, as if it was a poor second best: 'although we do go off mountaineering in Scotland now and then.'

Now even the slight traces of Yorkshire vowels had gone. Was it a useful affectation, that accent, Frank wondered.

'The stone beneath that gargoyle didn't seem very hard. Do you believe it was an accident, Simon?'

'Oh yes. I went up with Leon, no sign of any tampering at all. In Oxford the stone lasts for only about fifty years, you know. That must have stood there for five hundred. I call that pretty good.'

One fatality every half millennium? It's just a pity, Frank considered, that it nearly was me. But she persisted: 'Suppose someone *had* helped John Fisher's face on its way. They'd have been seen coming out of staircase E, wouldn't they?'

She'd already checked that the only Fellow with a room on E was Sir Barry Stone, who had been away in his lab at the time.

'No,' Simon assured her through a mouthful of Chinese delicacy. Chinese? Why had he wanted to come to a *Chinese* restaurant, the thought struck Frank. Oh come on, she chastised herself, I'm being ridiculous, losing my grip.

'No, there's a back door to each stair. For the servants, you know. Perfectly possible to slip out from the back of one staircase and come into the court from the front door of another.'

'Hey, Frank.' He laid chopsticks down and eyed her from under narrowed lids. Not lasciviously. Rather with complicity.

'Want to help me do a job tomorrow night? You look as if you'd have the right sort of build.'

'A job?' Frank hoped she didn't sound as bewildered as she was. 'What sort of job?'

'Just breaking and entering,' said Simon, as if it were a normal part-time occupation for English dons at ancient Cambridge colleges. Frank noticed that the Yorkshire accent had returned.

She felt like a pantomime stooge. 'Breaking and entering what?'

'I'd rather not say just now. You'll see if you come along. But,' he hastened to reassure her, as if that made it all right, 'it's not for money.'

Frank's open mouth was sufficient question.

'Secrets.' Simon brought his face down to direct the whisper straight at Frank, making sure none of the sibilance was lost in the remains of the platter of odd splayed toes on the table between them. 'There's some funny business going on around here and I aim to get to the bottom of it. Want to come along?'

Pasars, wondered Frank. It'd be a real break to be hired as spy's assistant.

'Most knew about it, I reckon.' Simon had now cupped hands over mouth. 'And that may be why they done him in.'

This was undoubtedly supposed to strike terror into Frank's heart. That organ in fact leaped for joy, but she contrived to keep a solemn face.

'All right Simon,' Frank agreed, in what she hoped was the right sort of intense, grave, conspiratorial tone, 'I'm on.'

'As long as there's no danger, mind,' she added, not wanting to appear too eager.

'No, you'll be all right with Simon, count on that. I'm an old hand at this sort of game.' And then without stopping for breath but with a sudden change from Yorkshire inflexions to best BBC: 'Come on then or we'll be late for the debate.'

It was clear that nothing more was to be said about 'the job' until eleven o'clock next evening. So, on the walk past haberdashers and ironmongers and chic expensive boutiques, Frank sought Simon's views on a different topic.

'Barry Stone tells me Delaney is favourite to be next Master, or so everyone was saying at breakfast.' Things do change quickly around here, she reflected.

Jeffrey halted abruptly outside Joshua Taylors. 'Barry *wants* him to be Master, that's what it is. No one was saying a thing at breakfast, we were all too sad about Most. Strewth, you don't think we're that heartless, do you?'

Sorry, thought Frank, and said: 'Why?'

'Well,' Simon assumed a patient tone for expounding the obvious, 'he really wants it himself, of course, but doesn't dare lose pride by being a candidate and turning out unsuccessful. Again.' Simon tapped his foot on the pavement. 'So if one can't be king the next best thing is to be king-maker. If you say a thing to enough people it is likely to happen, isn't that right.'

'Oh, undoubtedly,' Frank agreed. 'But *does* he want it? I mean the Kavendish might well be more exciting now than when Most was elected.'

'Yes, that is possible.' Simon looked at her sideways as they went up the passage towards the Arts Cinema. It seemed more and more likely that he did have some knowledge of Project Pasar. 'But he still wants to be king-maker.'

The debate really wasn't as interesting as it might have been. With a title like 'This house considers that America and Russia should be encouraged to blow each other up, then the rest of the world could live in peace' you might expect a scholarly tone tempered with a bit of invective. Not that there weren't eminent speakers. Dr Shivendra Krishnamurti, Secretary-General of the

United Nations, was a pretty good catch even for the wily Ms Bates, while the extreme right-wing British MP Dr John Tarry carried almost as much woomf.

But there weren't the sort of reasoned deliberate arguments one would surely expect from that sort of speaker on that kind of subject in that place. A few telling points but mostly mugging it up, playing to the gallery, scoring off one another—and the most dreadful English puns.

Everyone seemed to be there. At least almost everyone who had impinged on Frank during her twenty-seven hours in Cambridge. Well, a debate on nuclear power, more or less, would be expected to attract some of the Kavendish crowd. Sir Barry Stone seemed to be deep in conversation with Bernice Dodds, but then she moved away towards the back of the debating hall.

Sampson Ndagbera sat impassively, reading a bulky tome while waiting for things to begin. There was even the sallow face of Andrew's apple-selling groupee—well, he had been a student and maybe kept up membership of the Union. Delaney was down to speak third, for the motion, opposite Leon Ivanovitch. He hadn't mentioned this during their afternoon walk—you'd think Andrew might have needed that time to polish up his speech. Frank hoped he was all right after their narrow escape. Maybe sufficient combination room brandy would have done the trick.

Her worry had been misplaced, Frank decided, as the room rose in deference to the Presidential party. Louise strode in first, head held at a haughty height above her sequinned black dress. But still she was only about half the size of the tuxedoed Secretary whose long strides seemed to be phased in slow motion as he followed Louise up the side of the hall, ascended to the dais, and took his place in a plush armchair to the right of the Presidential throne. John Tarry stumbled twice—it could have been too much dinner wine, or the sudden bright lights, or simply an uneven hundred-year-old floor. Dr Shivendra Krishnamurti wore a wide grin, as if this were the proudest moment of his life. And so did Leon Ivanovitch—but then he usually did. Andrew Delaney came last, almost forgot to follow the rest, and the porter had gently to direct him to the right, up the aisle.

Andrew looked absent-minded, preoccupied, but really not shocked.

Simon had nobbled two places right at the end of the front row. Terrific view of John Tarry on the verge of falling asleep. Krishnamurti looked quite nervous. Leon pulled something out of his pocket—reprint of a scientific article?—and seemed about to read it, Ndagbera-fashion, until nudged by the supercilious Secretary.

Sundry items of official business. List of recent book purchases. The Librarian tried to be funny by reading *Finite Matrices* as if it were *Finite Mattresses* and commenting that the final chapter was titled 'Infinite mattresses'. Hearty good-natured guffaws from well-fed scions of English nobility, and those of lesser origin who hoped that three years at Cambridge was but the first step towards scaling the pyramid of British class.

John Tarry worked himself up into a paroxysm of excitement about very little. He wanted to send all the black people back to Africa or India or the West Indies, that became clear, but it wasn't obvious what relevance it had to the debate. Perhaps he'd come the wrong week?

'Why not transport all the Anglo-Saxons back to Scandinavia and leave England to the Welsh and the Cornish?' Frank extrapolated the line of argument further back in time, in a whisper at Simon's ear.

'The what?' he said, as if the idea of a Yorkshire cricket team centred on Malmo might be the only unacceptable consequence.

Tarry finally got to the point, which seemed to be that only Britain was fit to rule the world—to set decent standards of behaviour, don't you know. My God! Frank covered her face as wild cheers arose from one section of the gallery, only to be called to order by Louise's gavel. He'd have to get rid not only of Russia and America but France and Germany and Japan and China too, at the least, if England were again to become arbiter of world commerce, finance and justice.

After such stolid fascism Dr Shivendra Krishnamurti couldn't but sound like a paean of rationality. He began by listing all the times that the USA and USSR had helped the rest of the world, by non-militaristic aid, by advice, and by example. Camp David, hurrah.

'Why would an important man like Krishnamurti take time off to address a gaggle of students?' Frank enquired of Jeffrey.

The answer was simple. 'Krish was at Oxford. Spoke at the Union. Stood for President but never made it. *The Observer* said last week that it was the most severe setback he ever received. So this is like making up. Oxford never have invited him but we're the next best thing. Look at how the poor old ex-colonial is revelling in it.'

Frank forbore to say that India never was a colony. And in fact Krishnamurti's enjoyment was fast fading. The rabble on the balcony who had crowed over Tarry—had he brought them with him?—were now heckling Krish. In the UN he could have taken it. At a public meeting in Paris or New Delhi or Sydney he'd have been in total command of the situation. But here, on the podium at the Cambridge Union, the Secretary-General was plainly nonplussed.

Krishnamurti recovered composure as three sharp Presidential taps restored order. Frank saw he was now sweating heavily. The nuclear stockpile must be reduced. If all other nations put continual pressure on the leaders, even preferred to trade elsewhere, it must have some effect. Catcalls again: 'wouldn't listen to a pile of wogs.' Peaceful solution, Krishnamurti faltered as he read the last paragraph, was the only rational course. Any violent contest might mean the end of the world.

Heavy applause almost made up for the interruptions. Krish rose, to bow deeply to the hall, as Louise issued a stern reminder about the standards of behaviour which were expected in the Cambridge Union. Any further transgression and the culprit would be summarily ejected. Her six foot six Secretary sat up very straight and scowled at the gallery, as if he would be the one to carry out Presidential wishes on this matter.

It was left to Andrew Delaney to demonstrate true class. Surely an actual Cambridge Professor could argue logically, coherently—command the room to attention. The motion,

Delaney assumed, was meant to be somewhat metaphorical. Although it was theoretically possible for the two major powers to pepper each other's cities with minute atomic bombs, Hiroshima-size, and leave the rest of the world fairly intact, the most likely thing was that they would launch vast neo-neutron warheads with the result that all of Europe, and Canada and Mexico, and probably most—or quite possibly all—of the rest of the world would perish with them.

No, Andrew told a concentrating assembly, there were several ways in which the motion could be interpreted, none of them literal. Stop America and Russia having as much power. And this involved—he fixed a beady eye on Krishnamurti—changing or replacing the United Nations. That self-assured, haughty accent, Frank decided, was the main factor dividing Delaney and Krishnamurti. Indian English might be as socially acceptable in its own milieu as any other variety of the language—as her sociolinguistics lecturer at Chicago had insisted— but it was just a fact that Delaney's accent spelt aggressive self-confidence. An upper-class English voice simply was held in respect, everywhere.

Why should the power of veto be allowed to half a dozen nations chosen from hundreds. Russia and America. And England, he added. An attempt at a boo from Tarry's cohorts was quelled, instantly, by Delaney's direct steely gaze.

Another way of interpreting the motion was that the US and the USSR should be denied access to any new weaponry that might be developed in a more neutral country. Consider, Andrew invited the assembled students and dons and miscellaneous guests, consider a purely hypothetical situation. If, say, a wonderful new source of power were . . .

Tap, tap, tap. Louise gesturing at the clock. Delaney attempting to remonstrate, finding it not to accord with his dignity. Resignedly resuming his seat.

'He had only eight minutes,' Frank hissed at Simon. 'I thought each speaker was allowed ten?'

She received no answer as Dr Leon Ivanovitch, renowned physicist from Michaelhouse and the Kavendish, was introduced.

Formerly Director of the Soviet Nuclear Research Institute, he added, as if it were normal form to complete one's own description.

Great scientist Leon might be, but polished debater—no. How could anyone consider destroying Leon's beloved homeland, seemed to be the main gist. St Basil's Cathedral, gone for ever. Leon himself had been obliged to leave his wives—correction, wife—and children behind.

What pathetic mush, Simon mumbled, as Frank was tapped on the shoulder and handed a piece of paper. Folded. Sealed with scotch tape.

Leon was now into a joke. It seemed that there were originally only two TV channels in Moscow but that a new set came out with twenty, thirty channels.

The piece of paper was addressed FOR THE LADY WITH BLOND HAIR AND A YELLOW SWEATER AT THE LEFT-HAND SIDE OF THE FRONT. Lettered in square capitals—like a blackmail demand?

'They take the TV home. They switch on Channel One. It is Brezhnev delivering a lecture on the next five-year plan. Turn to Channel Two. Again Brezhnev, a homily on the sins of capitalism. Channel Three. This time Brezhnev talks of how grateful is Afghanistan. Channel Four, Brezhnev once more . . . and so it goes on.'

Frank could take her note home and open it there. She hesitated, tore at the tape, unfolded the sheet. Lined paper from a cheap exercise book.

'Channel Nineteen. Brezhnev on how grain production will be up this year. So once more turn the switch. Channel Twenty. There is the Chief of Police.' Leon waved a menacing finger at his audience and exaggerated his own accent: 'Stop changing channels!'

Noisy laughter. Applause. Leon sat down, bowing, blowing kisses into the hall.

Frank read the message once more. Neatly drawn capital letters. GO HOME YANK. And a skull and crossbones drawn in red below.

A joke? If there had been no poisoned drink or falling gargoyle that would have been Frank's first thought. From who? Not Leon, he was on the platform. The note would have been handled by many people on its way to her. No real hope of uncovering the source, in that crowded hall.

Undergraduates now spoke, better than their betters. There perhaps was some hope for the world, one eloquent girl from Clare argued, and Frank agreed, if there were enough like her, and less like John Tarry or Leon Ivanovitch. No—that was perhaps less than fair. Leon was a fine scientist, from that there seemed to be no dissent. He just should be protected from straying off his specialised path.

Why was Frank a threat? And to whom? She had so far discovered nothing, suspected no one. Unless there were something under her nose that she was too dumb to see. Never in six years of detective work had any situation made less sense to Frank.

Finally, the motion was carried by a majority of two to one. Time to go home. Frank steered Jeffrey right down the middle of Michaelhouse Court, well away from the trajectory of any large sculptured head. Simon's invitation to coffee in his room was tentative, perhaps expecting refusal. But with the presumption that it would be repeated, with more force next time, becoming increasingly difficult to decline.

Tiredness pulled at Frank but sleep was, for a while, unthinkable. Dance, think. Why did Louise cut off Delaney in full stride? What did he know, what had he been about to tell? What did Louise herself know? Dance. Slowly move body to mellow, mellifluous saxophone. Charlie Parker record. Rotate, extend, shiver and shimmy. A trumpet intruded, Dizzy Gillespie, cutting like a knife around the brown walls and floor. Like a knife to my heart, considered Frank, if I don't get somewhere fast.

V

Barry Stone drove a Porsche. It seemed a little grandiose for someone who prided himself, knighthood or not, on being a straightforward person—still the Queensland farm boy at heart, even though now thrust into the limelight of science.

At nine o'clock precisely he cruised up Trinity Street, stopped to allow Frank to snuggle into the front bucket seat. So, Sir Barry didn't always have breakfast in college. A boiled egg at home with Mrs Stone—correction, Lady Stone—in Barrow Road. What was it Andrew Delaney had said, with a tinge of aristocratic derision? That Sir Barry's wife was a plumber. Well, why not? Break down the sex barriers. Although, Frank admitted to herself, the idea of having one's washers renewed by Lady Stone was slightly priceless.

Sir Barry drove across Magdalene Bridge. A lorry had taken the corner off an overhanging first-floor casement, tudor-finished like something from a painting of Shakespearean England. The Porsche turned left, past a small market garden (right in the middle of Cambridge, potatoes and onions and peas for sale!). Churchill College, red bricks and white concrete slabs. Who'd want to go there in preference to a spooky room in King's or Corpus or Michaelhouse?

'Here we are.' Sir Barry came to a perfect halt exactly on the rectangle marked DIRECTOR. Kavendish with a K, Frank hummed to herself, like Lisa with a Zee. 'Soon find a room for you, no worries. Then I'll show you a bit of the geography of the place.'

'I've got a meeting at ten o'clock, though,' he added regretfully. 'Accelerator planning group. Delay-line detector trouble. You'd think they could manage position resolution as well as those fellows over in UCLA, wouldn't you?' Frank nodded in apparently sage agreement at the unthinkable incompetence of the Kavendish position resolvers, or whatever they were called.

She was given a tiny office, about the size of a cleaner's cupboard. A desk about two foot by three, one chair, a waste basket, and a blackboard on the wall. Next door to Leon Ivanovitch. Frank suddenly realised, with a mixture of apprehension and exhilaration, that his stentorian sing-song Russian voice could be heard, every word clearly audible through the pasteboard wall.

Quick tour of Lord Rutherford's old lab. The glassy metal group. Chests swelling with pride at the argon arc furnace that could produce metal crystals. Crystals of metal, Frank pondered. Oh that's a lovely engagement ring you have on my dear. Do let me see, what is the stone? Tin, oh lovely. I always think tin crystals cut so well, don't you?

Over the bowed-heads of furnace-worshipping scientists Frank spied a bicycle trundle past the window, a bicycle bearing Andrew Delaney, who did seem to have the knack of being almost everywhere that Frank was. Okay, so you couldn't really do math research more than three or four hours a day. But he hadn't done any yesterday afternoon, and probably wasn't this morning.

Stone's tour became quicker and quicker as ten o'clock approached. Electron-vibration interaction in hexavalent uranium. Man in charge looked like Professor Calculus from the Tintin stories, bald and beatific. Quick look in on Plasma Research. Hurry on to Gamma Ray spectroscopy where things were apparently just reaching an 'excited state'. Apt description, too, of Sir Barry.

Frank's request to be allowed to attend the meeting was given no thought at all. 'Do as you please.' But it really was terribly boring. How could people talk for close on two hours about chain idlers? Anyway, what was something with a name like that doing in a multi-million accelerator? Sounded more like an item out of a sawmill or tractor workshop.

Not knowing the first thing about physics, Frank had assured Sir Barry, would be a distinct advantage in her work. The aim was to see how people treated one another in the lab situation, how one spoke and the other responded. Not being able to comprehend what they were actually talking about would ensure there was no possibility of distraction from her study of interpersonal attitudes, antagonisms and anxieties.

One thing became clear as Sir Barry gradually brought everyone round to his point of view, that chain idlers were the critical flaw in the whole operation. The man was a politician. A combination of confidence and consistency, with a dash of good sense. How to win people over—flatter a little, and then take them while slightly off-guard, with powerful, insistent oratory. A man who could get his own way. Surely Barry Stone wouldn't have resorted to poison if, for whatever reason, he *had* wanted to rid the world of Patrick Most.

Just on eleven Andrew Delaney could be seen coming out of the wing that housed Ivanovitch and now also Frank. Mounting, wobbling, and then pedalling off bolt upright, sedately back to town. The Pasar team, Frank mused. One fairly assimilated Australian. One superficially westernised Russian. And an African PhD student. A British break-through, something that should be kept in England and denied the rest of the world, and there wasn't a Briton in sight? Perhaps that was fairly typical of the situation in England today, which was why John Tarry had such a following among the few pure-bloods that remained!

Louise Bates knew something of it, perhaps, and she was American. And Andrew Delaney? Frank didn't hold with women's intuition, but she did believe in detective's intuition. Something distinctly phoney about Professor Delaney. Not on the surface, like Simon Jeffrey's come-and-go Yorkshire accent. Delaney didn't quite ring true at a deeper level. Could the only Englishman in on the secret be the Chinese agent?

Lunch in the Kavendish canteen (why didn't the sign on the door say: Kanteen?). Notebook in hand, to write down names, make contacts. Everyone would be interviewed, at some time when whatever monstrous piece of equipment they cherished was puffing along happily on auto-drive. Which did seem, in fact, to be only a small proportion of the time. Like the Air Force's super-duper fighters, Frank reflected. Wonderful machines *when* they could be got in the air.

In-depth interrogation. Who do you work with? Who doesn't co-operate as much as they might? Which of the lab people do you see socially? It would be an interesting study in itself, Frank knew, and it might be decidedly useful in ferreting out where the Pasar leak could be situated.

'Mind if I join you?' Leon Ivanovitch and Louise Bates hadn't seemed to be exactly talking, which was unusual for both of them. Last night's Presidential finery had given way to denim jacket, denim jeans and the usual enormous heels, adding as much as possible to Louise's natural four foot ten.

'I enjoyed the debate,' Frank began, and by Leon's slight grimace sensed what had been the source of friction. Well, just because the motion was passed didn't really mean that we all wished Russia to be removed from the map. She wanted to pat him on the back and tell him.

Frank had chosen a 'minute steak' but couldn't decide whether it was 'minute' as in 'sixty seconds' or 'minute' as in 'very small'. Better anyway than Leon's rissoles which he had pushed away. 'I must now go and pretend to work some more, as my witty colleagues say.'

Which left Frank and Louise. Black and white. Harvard, since they started taking in gifted representatives of minority groups, and Vassar, which really hadn't. Although Louise, on closer inspection, didn't look entirely WASP. Her eyes . . . hint of Red Indian?

'I really admire the way you get such interesting speakers to the Union, and to talk on really relevant issues.' Frank meant it. She didn't add that what they had to say on them was pretty dull.

A thaw was noticeable. 'Why, thanks.' Then followed words of platitude. Enquiry about Frank's role. Interest. Promise to help, perhaps genuine.

'The Kavendish must be an exciting place to work,' Frank hazarded. 'I mean this is where they split the atom which is surely *the* most important scientific breakthrough this century. Or perhaps ever?'

'And,' she continued, 'a breakthrough of the same importance might happen again at any time. Surely?' An innocuous enough suggestion, she hoped. Naïve. Romanticising. No clue that Frank had a glimmer of what was happening. Of Pasar power, Pasar planes, Pasar spaceships. And Pasar bombs.

Close observation of Louise. A pause, momentary. (And it wasn't the bit of gristle she had encountered in the rissole.) Slight furrowing of brow. Then large, sweeping friendly response. 'Yes, Frank, it is exciting. But also lots of hard work. Splitting the atom could only happen once in the history of science. I don't think anything like that is likely to recur. Not anything with the same consequences for world peace.'

That wasn't what I said, thought Frank. And the denial was too glib, too definite. There seemed little doubt that Louise should figure prominently on the list of suspects. Stone, Ivanovitch, Ndagbera—the Pasar team. Andrew Delaney and Louise Bates. Lord Johns and anyone else in the government who was in on the secret. Simon Jeffrey? Quite possibly. Patrick Most, who was now dead, and his chic de facto Dr Bernice Dodds, who most decidedly wasn't.

Frank left the canteen and walked slowly towards her office. Project Pasar was the only one that Sir Barry had not exhibited that morning. Those 200 pages of Pasar theory. Someone, said Lord Johns, was slipping copies to the Chinese. For money? Because of political idealism? Out of spite—personal or professional? Why? Why the Chinese? Of course, Frank reflected, they probably did have more need of a quick cheap power source than any other nation. And would they make sensible use of it? Why not?

Three quick knocks on the door beyond Leon's. 'Come in,' said an educated voice, lacking the astringency of Stone, the affectation of Delaney. Sampson Ndagbera was wearing a grey suit, attired more neatly than any scientist Frank had met that morning. He sat in a room the size of Frank's, three sharp pencils on the desk, neat, spidery formulas on the pad before him. One crossed out, another below it. Full of Σs and ∞s and σs and ϕs.

'Yes, I am glad to meet you Miss le Roux.' It wasn't exactly a stammer, more a sharp intake of breath before a stressed syllable—h'Roux. But Ndagbera's mouth seemed to open a fraction too soon, hesitate, and you wondered at first if he was going to succeed in saying the word.

'Barry told me about your study and I'll be glad to help. Sounds really—h'fascinating.' Frank had an impression of extraordinary dignity.

'Polite' would be too crude a word. Natural grace, serenity, confidence and yet—not exactly meekness. Deference? Not that either. Something held back, unspoken, perhaps waiting to blossom forth when the time should be ripe.

Sampson and Frank had two small rooms with one chair each. Why not a walk in the May sunshine? 'Good idea to take advantage while it's here. May be the last sun we see all summer,' Sampson suggested, talking from his experience of two cold, grey, damp Cambridge years.

Across Madingley Road. Along a narrow footpath, only just room to walk abreast. Frank began by volunteering some biography. Born in New Orleans, hot and sweaty and subject to inundating floods. Grade school in the French Quarter. Holidays with father, catching alligators and hiding from customs men in the cypress-fringed bayous. North to college. And now, her first time in Cambridge, England.

Sampson responded quite naturally. First establish who one is talking to. Background, points of common experience and interest. 'I come from Nigeria. You remember h'Biafra?' Frank nodded. 'My people, the Igbo, we have always valued our independence.'

They turned away from the noise of cars and lorries, which drowned out every third sentence. To the left, along a grassy track towards the University Observatory. 'The Igbo never had any kings,' Sampson continued. 'Europeans brought gifts and gave them to the head man of the first village. Then the chief in the next village wanted attention too. We had a thousand villages all living together in one Igbo h'nation. Plenty of food. Men and women worked together in the fields. Yams and h'taro and cassava.'

Sounds like paradise, thought Frank. Australian Aborigines had no rulers but they did practise a strict division of labour between the sexes. Men hunted; women gathered vegetables and firewood, built the huts, cooked the food, minded the children—the same old story. But the Igbos—wasn't this what China was working towards? Real Marxism.

'What sort of things did your people use for trade, Sampson? What did they export?'

A moment's thought. Then an honest answer. 'Palm oil. And h'slaves.'

Well, decided Frank, the illusion was good while it lasted.

The Astronomy Department was situated in an old house. Maybe a Professor's residence from the last century, and he'd drive each day in to college by sulky. Frank realised she was just romancing (and why not?). Now earnest scientists could be seen through the windows, punching data into a computer.

'I would still be there now, getting cassava,' Sampson explained, 'if it had not been for a missionary. From the h'Wycliffe Bible Translators. Learning to read, that is the most important thing, did you ever think of it?' Frank had to admit, to her shame, that she hadn't. 'Without that skill I should be at most an important man in my h'village. But once I can read, every avenue is open to me. There is always a book which will explain how to do something, h'where to go, who to ask.'

'Your mathematics, though,' Frank enquired. 'Andrew Delaney told me you worked it all out for yourself. You didn't need teaching.'

Ndagbera shrugged as they now ventured on to another path. Branches looping over their heads and roots extruding up through the ground covering of leaves and bark and cherry blossom. 'There must be something to build on. There were books on Algebra and Calculus at the University in Ibadan. I just took those principles and applied them further . . .'

'And your teachers there were so impressed that they sent you on to Cambridge.' Frank supplied the happy ending.

'No,' Sampson took off his jacket, folded it neatly over his arm. 'They were not sufficiently clever to understand my work. My grades were just enough to h'pass. But I sent the theorems I had proved to mathematicians in England.'

'To Andrew Delaney?' This time Frank restricted herself to a cautious query.

'To two other famous professors first. They did not reply. Then h'Delaney did, and here I am.'

They had reached a sign which announced 'The University Farm'. Sampson Ndagbera crouched down beneath an elm tree. Pulled from his pocket a handful of peanuts. Peered up into the tree, and made a soft clicking push of tongue against gums. One grey squirrel head came tentatively into view, checking. Reassured, it scrambled down in a single movement and stood by a protruding flange, accepting and eating nuts at a slightly faster rate than Ndagbera could profer them.

Frank watched, fascinated.

'This squirrel is me.' Sampson looked at her quite seriously. 'Some people in Cambridge—not in Michaelhouse, but in the town—think of anyone with a black skin as like a monkey in a tree. Not quite a human being. I get a scholarship to study at Cambridge. Gather morsels of your civilisation. Then I shall return, home, to the tree-tops.'

'But surely, Sampson,' Frank remonstrated, 'you could get a permanent Fellowship here? Any college would have you.'

A nod to indicate agreement. 'But why should I stay here, in an alien place, where I am not wanted?' A second handful of nuts as he added: 'And not h'loved.'

'Yes, obviously you should go back to your own country.' Frank somehow felt, even when talking to Ndagbera, that she was still one step behind. They reached the end of the path. Turned into Storey's Way. Fifty yards, walk around a red postbox, as if that were Sampson's regular ritual, and return.

'The work you're doing with Leon and Sir Barry must be pretty exciting?' Frank hazarded. 'Will it be any use to your people in Nigeria?'

Sampson's normally impassive face suddenly burst into a grin. 'It might make us all equal,' he blurted out. 'If my people have cheap power, if they can farm the land efficiently, if we do not rely on foreign capital. If we can kick—' he aimed a foot, in polished brown leather shoe, at a twisty root across the path, '—if we can kick h'Coca Cola out of Africa. If we can look after our own lives, our work, our play. Then we need no longer be aware that we are black.'

If Frank hadn't known about Pasars all this would have been totally incomprehensible. Sampson, normally so alert, seemed here unaware. Or perhaps he knew, instinctively, that she was in on the secret.

'Yes, I know what you mean,' Frank sympathised, 'about being black.'

'How can you?' Sampson looked at her with astonishment.

'Well,' said Frank, looking at her arms, which could have belonged to a native of Cyprus, or Sicily. 'I am black.'

'That is to say,' she hurriedly hastened to add, 'I count as black. My great-grandfather was a black cornet player.' It suddenly all seemed so inconsequential. He blew a white man's instrument, and often played for the whites, at southern picnics. 'His grandfather came from Africa,' she desperately added.

'Pah!' All hint of stammer was now lost. 'You do not know what it is like to be scowled at. To be ignored in a shop—yes, in Cambridge. To have people mutter and giggle behind your back in a cinema queue. You can choose. No one would question it if you claimed to be white. For you "being black" is an indulgence. For me it is reality.'

Frank chose not to reply. For shame, in part, that Sampson had described her life so accurately. Like the time in South Africa when Frank had stayed in whites-only hotels, eaten in whites-only restaurants, drunk in whites-only bars. How else would she have been able to pierce a thousand-million-dollar diamond smuggling operation, spanning four continents, two members of the American President's cabinet, one French Minister, and two most highly placed British diplomats? But Sampson Ndagbera would not have had that option open to him.

'I'm sorry,' Sampson broke the silence. 'I know that you meant well. It is just that this is a sensitive issue to me. And,' he added, looking across Madingley Road at the white box-like building over which Sir Barry Stone reigned, 'things have been hectic at the lab recently.'

He hesitated. Frank, who had grasped his arm as they crossed the road just behind a large green bus, gave a gentle squeeze. 'An exciting breakthrough. Which might change my country, as I was telling you. But things are not simple. They are never simple. Pressures, you know.'

Frank stopped her mind gyrating over things like: money from the Chinese to get the capital to actually develop Pasar power in Nigeria. She thanked Ndagbera for the walk.

A hesitant invitation to have dinner with him one day. Monday? Yes, Frank said she would look forward to that. And she *would*, in at least two quite different ways.

Time for half an hour in her wee office before the promised lift back to Michaelhouse in the Directorial Porsche. Notes of the meeting that morning, of lunch, of Sampson's black complex. Black? Something was different. On the blackboard, before Frank's eyes for the past ten minutes. A message; neatly lettered in capitals. Two lines.

BEWARE OF DEATH
SHE STRIKES BUT ONCE

Phew, and just as I'd been thinking we'd gone a whole nineteen hours without a drop of poison or a large lump of falling stone, or a folded note. Whatever Sampson says there is one advantage to being illiterate, Frank ruminated, as she sat and stared at the message.

VI

'THING TO DO is get a second-hand bike.' A gentle hint from Sir Barry Stone, as he dropped her off at the front gate of Michaelhouse, that the chauffeur service wouldn't continue indefinitely. 'If you're going to spend a couple of months with us, that is.'

'But there's no hurry,' he added, so as not to appear unfriendly, 'not for a few days yet anyway.'

Provided I live through the next few days, Frank made a private bargain with herself, I'll buy a spanking new bicycle. Fast, sporty, ten-gear. And red, yes definitely, red.

She was first in the combination room. Time to catch up on a bit of news. Front page headline: 'America accuses Russia of clandestine arms build-up.' Tell us something new. Frank turned to the middle page of *The Times*. She was always fascinated by Court News, especially the bit about Ladies-in-Waiting. What do they do? Just wait, and wait, and wait, while the Queen makes up her mind which dress to wear?

A sober double-column heading on the right-hand side of page twelve. 'OBITUARIES: Dr Patrick Most, Master of Michaelhouse.' Frank settled down to enjoy the expert turn-of-phrase. As much as one can enjoy reading of the death of a man who one met two days before, and to whom one handed the potion that poisoned him. Not even properly blessed, either.

'Dr Most,' the anonymous correspondent reported, 'never fully realised his early promise as a linguist, devoting himself more to questions of how grammars should be written, than to the actual description of languages. He constantly regretted the rate at which rare tongues were proceeding to extinction without being sufficiently documented . . .'

There were some kind phrases about Most's Mastership: 'His

uncanny knack of being familiar with the priorities of each Fellow and ensuring that . . .'

'And you were impressed with our great laboratory, no?'

'Well, yes.' Dr Leon Ivanovitch seemed to have crept into the room and suddenly his head appeared a foot from Frank's, following her gaze on to the newspaper, which she almost dropped in surprise. 'Yes indeed, what I saw was fascinating.'

But I didn't smell the merest whiff of Pasars, she intended to imply. Ivanovitch ignored this bait. 'Those amorphous metals, aren't they wonderful. Just like glass. Now, how about a glass of sherry? Dry?'

'You must know more about Cambridge than I. Talking to so many people,' Leon continued, handing Frank her glass with a smiling bow. 'Louise and Sampson and that Simon Jeffrey.' He settled low into an armchair, dirty boots on a seventeenth-century inlaid rosewood table. 'Getting the sociological round-about on the place. Is that right?'

'Lowdown,' Frank corrected, and Leon nodded as if what he had said were entirely equivalent.

'Louise. You would have much in common with her.'

'Would I?' wondered Frank.

'Not in personality, of course.' One huge Ivanovitch boot was scraped along the bevelled edge of the table, removing a layer of mud and one embedded pebble. 'But physically, is what I intended. You have one Negro grandfather and she has one Chinese grandfather.'

Great-grandfather, and we stopped using a derogatory term like Negro more than fifteen years ago. Frank's correction was purely mental. So Louise had Chinese ancestry. That would explain the slightly oriental look. But was it enough to make her a spy? Well, something had to be enough to make someone a spy around here!

Leon actually did place his feet on the floor as more Fellows entered. Dark monogramed ties, sports jackets and gowns contrasting with Ivanovitch's zippered open-neck windcheater. Well, if the lady students didn't have to wear a tie why should the gentlemen students? And if they didn't why should the émigré

Russian Fellow? Leon did, of course, sport a gown, marked here and there with memories of previous meals.

In the absence of Barry Stone, Dr Primitive Procreation led them into hall and sat at the head of the table. Not the middle, where Most had presided at the Ffothergill-Hawthorn-Williams affair, but the left-hand end, right under John Fisher. Frank felt that she'd recently had quite enough of being under, or almost under, John Fisher, but the invitation to sit next to Bernice plainly could not be declined.

Frank realised that although she seemed to have been at Cambridge for about ten times as long as she actually had—two-and-a-bit days, was that all?—this was her first normal High Table dinner. But not Bernice's. Although she seemed oddly lacking in know-how by inviting the head waiter to serve Frank first. That gallant was now dressed merely smartly, like someone at Sardi's; the red carnation from Feast night must have wilted away.

He respectfully declined. 'Whoever sits in that chair,' he indicated Bernice's position at the end of the long, dark table, 'must be served first. By tradition.'

Good-oh, Frank decided. She gets to taste the soup and sip the wine before me. In view of having been almost murdered twice, and having received two threatening notes (the last of which, at least, appeared to be somewhat serious) Frank had embarked on a course of caution. Life, for the saving of, one, to wit: F. le Roux.

'The Mastership.' Frank gingerly edged into an important topic. 'When is the election, Dr Dodds?'

'Bernice,' corrected Mrs Ethnic Kinsey. 'Wednesday. Must be within a week of the—er—death. By statute, you know.'

Frank wondered if it might be too delicate a matter to plumb information on candidates from one who was so—ah—closely—ah . . . She need not have worried. Dr Dodds volunteered a survey of the field as if she were giving a lecture on kin relations among the Eskimos.

'La ronde, well, almost.' Bernice articulated the facts lightly, precisely, between spoonfuls of delicate, almost-red consommé. 'Barry Stone fancies Delaney. I think it's because he has the traditional Australian hero-worship of the mother country, and Andrew so perfectly personifies the extreme intellectual conservative.'

I know what you mean, Frank went along. The Aussies say they loathe unctuous Britishness but they really dote on it. Andrew is okay by his accent, but surely you know he's also a rabid Marxist. Funny sort of combination. Frank supposed that Burgess and Philby were much the same, although they must have kept their political sympathies a little better hidden.

'Andrew says he wants Leon!' Bernice tested the wine. Burgundy. Only about ten years old. Approved. Her glass was filled to a regulation half inch from the rim.

'Why?' Frank took care to request the same bottle, although she really would have preferred white.

'He considers it might be a lot of fun.' Bernice unbent a little, lent over towards Frank. 'Can you imagine the undergraduates being exhorted to greater effort by a solecistic harangue from Leon? And,' she added, as if it were overall the most important consideration, 'he is developing quite a respectable palate.'

'What about Leon?' prompted Frank.

'Leon wants Lord Johns. You know how Russians are? A bit like Americans. People who haven't got any nobility of their own. They just love anything like a Lord.'

Pretty sweeping generalisation. Maybe that's why your book sells so well, Frank ruminated, if it's based on gross induction of that order.

Bernice's head was now almost touching Frank's. 'Leon once went to lunch at Imperial College, and they asked him to sign the visitors' book. There was a column headed "title", you know, Dr or Professor or Ms. Do you know what Leon wrote there?'

Frank shook her head. She suspected she wouldn't care, anyway.

'He wrote "Earl",' Bernice concluded triumphantly, with a mixture of admiration and outrage. 'Earl Ivanovitch, can you beat that?'

Roast turkey appeared. A plate of vegetables hovered at the right height for Frank to help herself. With spoon and fork, apparently both held in the same hand, somewhat like chopsticks.

'And I would rather like it for myself,' Bernice added in total honesty. 'I quite fancy the job.'

But she didn't say why. Observing the sexual habits of undergraduates? Comparing the relative success rates of the Grantham Grope and the Loughborough Lunge?

'I was reading in *The Times*,' Frank interposed, 'that Dr Most was interested in the East.'

'Yes,' Bernice agreed, 'he was fascinated by it. Just over the past few years. Their approach to science. He always said he'd like to learn Chinese but couldn't find the time. Poor thing.'

'So it was China in particular?'

'Oh yes, indeed. Patrick had no time for the Japanese.' Bernice flushed, as if at some geishaesque reminiscence. 'And that's why he got on so well with Lord Johns—who has a degree in Chinese history, you know.'

Frank didn't. In fact she'd thought that it was in medicine. What the heck, his Lordship had lived long enough to do a few things, and China did seem to be looming rather large. Louise had a yellowish grandfather. Most and Lord Johns doted on the place. Delaney was a rip-roaring Marxist and Leon used to be. Only Sampson Ndagbera hadn't mentioned it. Oh, and nor had Simon Jeffrey.

Frank looked down the table to where Simon was deep in discussion with Derek Randall, Michaelhouse's sharp-nosed historian.

It was Delaney who caught her eye. 'Hey, Frank. Want to come on the river tomorrow afternoon. In a punt. See how the idle rich spend their Saturdays?'

'Yes, sure.' It sounded pleasant, and Delaney was certainly someone who required further study.

'Two o'clock,' the Professor of Pure Mathematics confirmed, 'and Sampson'll come along too.'

After dinner there was a couple of hours for Frank to curl up in the privacy of her room with a book, from the pile so thoughtfully provided for guests of the college. The biography of Rutherford palled after a while. So he could make physics apparatus from paper clips and rubber bands, so what? *The Masters* by C. P. Snow was much more absorbing. Indeed, she had only just remembered to change into dark burglary-suited clothes—brown corduroy trousers, black sweater, black silk scarf over blond hair, no earrings lest they might glisten in the moonlight or in a searchlight—when a sharp double-knock on the door, eleven o'clock precisely, announced the arrival of burglar-in-chief, Dr Simon Jeffrey, expert on Dr Johnson, and on gathering secrets. From the Kavendish—perhaps. . . .

Bang on. 'I might as well tell you we're going to the Kavendish,' he began. 'Synchronise watches!'

'Why?' demanded Frank. 'Are we going separately?' And you steal away while I get caught. No fear. Let's get all that straight at the beginning.

'Oh no,' Jeffrey reassured her. And shrugged, as if to say: well don't you know they always synchronise watches, in books and films and things. 'Don't worry, come on.'

He made a distinctly sinister figure: black skull cap, black sweater, trousers and shoes and a bulky black bag slung from his shoulder, from which came the most amazing smell. Frank hurried him down the stairs before her room came to pong like a—yes, like a slaughterhouse, that was exactly it.

Simon slunk around the side of the court, let them out of a side gate with a key to which presumably he was entitled. Ran his flashlight up and down Frank. Then along the bicycle rack. 'Try this one for size,' he invited, simultaneously with slipping off a four-digit combination lock. Thirty seconds it had taken him, at most.

'Whose is it?' Frank was able to venture as she perched on the saddle, toes just touching ground.

'Doesn't matter.' Jeffrey was now liberating another bicycle, for his own use. Checking the tyres.

When Sir Barry Stone said I really ought to get a bike I don't think he quite meant this way. 'Will we bring them back?' Frank asked, thinking of some distraught student unable to cycle off to the nether end of Cambridge for a nine o'clock lecture.

'We might, doesn't matter. Don't concern yourself with details,' Jeffrey commented as he mounted, swung bag across back, and began pedalling towards Trinity Street.

Frank had intended at this point getting clear *why* they were going there, *what secret* in the Kavendish, what Simon would *do* with it *when* he got it. But her co-conspirator's dark shape was fast receding as Simon got up a nice rhythm on his borrowed bike. Along Trinity Lane, turn right towards the river. Phew, no lights, Frank had almost lost sight of the shadowy figure in front but followed a just perceptible squeak, squeak. Silly Simon, he should have brought along a can of oil.

A steep hump-back bridge over the Cam. Frank felt her knee about to give way and got off, pushing the purloined cycle to the top. Simon was hunched over the bridge. 'Sorry. I should've realised you'd not be used to cycling.' Not for ten years, Frank thought, since I used to ride each day to High School, a clean T-shirt to change into when I got there.

A punt drifted by below, muted giggle from huddled couple as the current gently propelled them downstream.

'You go first,' suggested Simon.

'But where to?'

'Straight on. Over the road. Then Burrell's Walk past the library, cross another street and straight down Adams Road. Stop when you get to the end. T-junction, you can't miss it. I'll be just behind.'

It had all seemed at first like an undergraduate prank, some sort of parody of the real thing. Simon now led the way, more slowly, from a sign which read 'Footpath to Coton'. Approach from the back. Of course one should approach from the back. But surely a professional would do that. The way in which Simon acted—decisive, confident, determined—did make it seem more and more as if he was something of an expert at this sort of lark. As if it were, in truth, not a lark at all.

A high wire fence, seven foot at the least, appeared on the right.

'Okay, leave your bike here. Don't forget to lock it up. Your combination is 2777.'

It wasn't meant to be questioned but Frank did respond, in the same low voice, not quite a whisper: 'Why? They aren't even ours.'

'Look Frank, we'll need them to get home again.'

Which was true, and they might well be in a hurry.

'Anyway,' Simon concluded the argument, 'they've been pinched once tonight. We don't want it to happen again, do we?'

Frank did as she was told, although there didn't seem too much chance of a prowler who might fancy a stray bike. The middle of Cambridge was just about deserted by eleven o'clock. Out here it could have been the middle of the Mojave desert.

Simon's arm was just about to disappear into the mysterious foul-smelling, clanking bag when Frank restrained it. 'Simon, we need to talk a minute. Tell me what we're going for.'

'I don't know.' He shrugged off her hand and began rummaging. 'They've got some secret in the Kav. I know they have. Lots of whispering in corners and suchlike. And I aim to share in it. After all I pay my taxes, don't I? Why shouldn't I see what all that lolly gets spent on?'

Was it just a case of Simon liking a bit of adventure and this being the only thing he could think of at the moment? But, after all, if he *were* about to sell the secret Frank couldn't really expect to be told, like that.

A rolled bundle was extracted. Tied up. Simon sat down to unravel it in the darkness. Just a thin new moon—had that been part of the plan?

'You've done this sort of thing before?' Frank ventured.

'Look,' the Yorkshire brogue exaggerated Jeffrey's slight impatience, 'my uncle was the top burglar in Bradford. Did all the nobs, he did, once a year, regular as clockwork. Pictures, jewellery, booze, money. Even started taking TV sets towards the end. But he said they were too heavy, that was what convinced him it was time to retire.'

'And you . . .?'

'Sure, I helped him. You've got to have someone to keep a look-out, help carry the swag, haven't you?' A warm tone engulfed Dr Jeffrey's memories of the halcyon days of his youth.

'He was a good sort, Uncle Mose. And a terrific teacher. Everything I know about this game comes from him.'

Frank wanted to ask what Simon's father and mother had thought of their son's education. Whether they had known—perhaps sent him along to learn a useful trade. Had he received a share of the loot? Was Simon's dad a forger, say, or a respectable clerk?

There was no time. The rope ladder had been unrolled, thrown over the fence. Dull bang as metal weights on one end hit against far side of fence. There was a rectangle of leather in the centre and Simon wriggled his end until it rested squarely over the top.

'There,' he said proudly, 'just the job. I had to sew a couple of feet into it. Bit bigger this than the last job.'

Frank had an image of Dr Jeffrey sitting before a roaring fire in his college study. A student in one armchair, reading his weekly essay on something like animal imagery in eighteenth-century English novels, while Simon sat listening, nodding sympathetically, adding a new metaphor here and there, and all the while stitching at his ladder, putting in a couple of extra rungs on each side, testing to see if they were strong enough.

'You go over first, Frank, and I'll hold it this end. Here—take my bag will you? Just drop it on the ground the other side.'

The bag banged against Frank's hips as she cautiously ascended the rope ladder. Seemed to squirm—surely it didn't contain a live animal? There were also hard bits, protruding at odd angles, that made it hard to manipulate over the top of the fence. Why the hell couldn't Simon have carried it over himself?

Getting the ladder back took longer. Frank pulled gently, while Simon put his hands through the fence, wrapped one around each rising weight so that they did not clang on the horizontal bars. Then a quick flip over the top, to the right while Frank crouched off left. No good getting clonked on the head at this stage.

'Why don't we leave it here for getting away again?' This time Frank did use a whisper. There were lights on in the building, now only thirty yards away.

'Someone might notice. I expect to be inside several hours, you see.'

My God, thought Frank. All she could say was: 'Simon, are you sure there's no risk in all this?'

He didn't understand the question quite as it had been intended. 'No, not really. The secret is, don't carry a gun. Burglary with firearms we might get five years. But if you're not armed it'll be six months, first offence.'

He quickly rolled up the ladder, popped it back into bag. 'Fifty-fifty chance we could say it was a student jape and get off with probation,' Simon continued. 'But of course there'd be no chance at all of that if you carried a gun.'

Creep up towards the next fence. Suddenly Simon broke the silence: 'You don't have a gun, do you Frank?'

'Oh no,' she agreed, untruthfully. Don't think. Concentrate on the task in hand. Next fence was only five foot. Get over without a ladder? She extended a hand to test horizontal strip of wire as foothold.

'Don't!' Simon Jeffrey slapped Frank's hand away so roughly that she almost lost balance. Instinctively she made as if to hit him back.

'It's electrified,' he hissed, shining a pinhole of light on a flat red metal sign that remarked on 24,000 volts.

Thick rubber gloves out of bag. Pliers with long rubber grips. Roll of wire with a clip at each end. Snap it on to the top strand. If that was the only strip that was live then Frank hadn't really been in danger.

'Stay there!' he ordered. Frank had never felt more rooted to any spot. About two feet from the fence.

Simon simply walked around her, paying out his coil of wire very slowly a yard beyond Frank. Then, the circle completed, he clipped the other end on to the fence, ten feet away from the first clip.

What good does that do? Frank wondered. We're now in a small circle of electrified wire. Can't move forward, can't go back, unless you fancy jumping in the dark over 24,000 volts.

With his pliers Simon now cut the top strand of wire right in front of them. Tested with small piece of wood taken from magical bag.

'Quite safe. Over you go.' Frank pulled herself up. Luckily electric current was held to be enough without the added luxury of barbed wire.

Simon grasped her thigh to help steady, and push. Frank had a sudden urge to kick him in the balls, bash knee into throat. Better not. She'd need Simon for getting back, for one thing. And this really was rather exciting. Well-researched, well-prepared, well-executed. Uncle Mose sure had known his profession.

'Aren't you going to take the wire off, Simon?'

'How?' A patient answer. Well yes, it would be a bit tricky from this side. Sort of a silly question.

'Don't worry,' Mose's nephew explained. 'No one could possibly see it. The main thing is that we haven't broken the current. That really would have set the cat among the pigeons. Triggers off an automatic alarm here which is connected to one at the Cambridge Police Station and another at the nearest RAF base.'

'How did you . . . ?' But Frank's question had been anticipated. 'I chat to the security men in the pub. How else would you find out things like that?' How else indeed? And with Simon's Yorkshire front surely no one would take him for an academic. Or a part-time high-class burglar. Or a Chinese spy? Well, if his second string didn't any longer seem absurd, why should the third?

Rubber gloves and pliers could now be stowed away. It suddenly occurred to Frank that if Simon had wanted to get rid of her he could just have allowed a touch of the last fence. Dr Jeffrey disappears back to college and there lies Ms le Roux, late investigating agent, sadly electrocuted while trying to penetrate the Kavendish. For English secrets, by Gawd.

It suddenly occurred to Frank that she hadn't yet sounded out Simon's opinion. They were now moving forward very slowly towards the last fence. What a contrast from driving in that morning in Stone's Porsche, attendant saluting at open gate.

'Simon, who do you fancy for Most's job?'

He didn't take it as at all an odd time for election news. 'Oh, Delaney, I'd think . . .'

They both froze. Frank grasped his arm, squeezed tight. A low growl came from over the last fence. Almost too low to be heard by human ears. Quivering, menacing, a deep canine growl that spoke of sharp teeth, an empty stomach and no mercy.

'Quick.' Simon did seem flustered as he fumbled in the bag. Extracted a polythene sack with something soft and red inside. Tore at the wrapping with his teeth, blood splattering on to the ground, probably on to the bag. (None on Frank, she thought.) Large piece of raw red meat. Tipped over the fence. Alsatian jaws chomping, threatening stance replaced by satisfied licking of lips.

'What—' Frank began, a little too loud. The lighted windows were now only about ten yards distant.

'Poison.' Simon put a finger to his lips.

'But . . . but when they find a dead dog, in the morning?'

'No dead dog.' His mouth against her ear. 'Not really poison. Powerful anaesthetic. Six hours and Fido'll be right as rain. All the better for a good feed and a good sleep. Just gives us time to get in and out.'

Up till then it had been sheer skill, Frank admitted. But now, surely a huge slice of luck. Just one good loud bark and . . . ? It would have taken them at least twenty minutes to reach the bicycles again. But, she reflected, what else could Simon have done? Short of shooting the dog, and that would certainly have left a message.

Frank climbed over the third fence followed by her boss burglar, his bag now lighter but with an unfortunate tendency to clank. The dog lay stretched out on the grass, ribbons of meat extending from incisors which were the size of small horns. It must have stood four feet tall. Frank shivered.

'The hardest part's to come. Don't relax!'

Never had Frank le Roux received a warning that was more unnecessary. Fighting side-by-side with guerillas in Afghanistan, pretending to be a French voyeur just below the poppy triangle, talking to Marxists in Chile—these were like a Sunday

School picnic compared to secret-stealing with Dr Simon Jeffrey. Which worthy now sidled up to the building, slowly round to the darkest side where he extracted, from bag, a chunky bunch of keys. Uncle Mose's?

'Cleaners arrive at 6 am,' Simon advised, while turning over keys like beads on a rosary, searching for the right size. 'Just one watchman here at night. Supposed to walk around twice every hour but that's a bit variable.' One key put into lock. Won't turn. Try another. 'Twice a week more like it, I've been told.'

In the pub, Frank added to herself.

'Unless there's any scientists working late,' he added, as the second key was also rejected.

Those windows. Frank suddenly orientated the geography of the building. There'd been time for careful observation that morning. Frank's father, she resolved, could pace Uncle Mose when it came to seeing the lie of the land, working out just what went where and why and what direction the customs agents were most likely to appear from.

She did a double-check. No doubt at all. Lights had been on in the rooms assigned to Sampson Ndagbera and Leon Ivanovitch—left at dinner two hours before, more than slightly drunk. And the third light had been in the office assigned to Frank le Roux, agent hired by Her Majesty's Government to discover—quickly, quietly and discreetly—just who was smuggling away Project Pasar. If anyone was. Hell!

Third key turns smoothly in heavy iron lock. Simon holds door open. Ladies first! Even when burgling?

'Simon,' hand on his arm. 'You saw there were lights on over in the west side. That's where—' Frank just stopped herself saying: that's where the Pasar team work. 'That's where we might want to go.'

'Dead right,' he agreed. 'Stone's office. That's where the secrets are. Must be.'

Creeping around corridors with pin-hole light. Laboratory One, the sign read, Plasma Research. Stop at corner, corridor ahead dark and empty. Laboratory Four, Amorphous Metals Research. Next corner, south-west of building. This was the vital wing. Break-through that would change the face of the earth. Transistors? Lasers? Pah—put away your toys. Pasars will heat a town for twenty dollars a year, send a rocket to Alpha Centaurus in months or weeks. Two hundred and fifteen pages of Pasar Theory, Sir Barry Stone had confided inside the soft pink curtains of his four-poster. One hundred and sixty-two of them existed in several copies, lying around bedrooms in Michaelhouse College. And in offices in the Kavendish, no doubt. But the vital fifty-three pages were in Sir Barry's safe. Here, in the Director's room. The combination known only to one man, an Australian sheep-farmer's son who now had the future of the world in his palm, more or less. Irrigation would be easy. Processing, delivering, marketing—a cinch. Surely not the whole cure for the world's ills. The birth-rate might require a bit of attention. And—let it never disappear from my mind for one instant, Frank reminded herself—conflict will still occur. Jealousies, intrigues, ancient feuds could be more powerful than ever, and a thousand times bloodier, with Pasar power.

Lights would be expected to shine through glass panels on doors. Lights from three rooms, visible ten minutes before. No longer visible. The Pasar corridor was as dark and empty and eerie as each other part of Cambridge's premier laboratory.

'They're gone!' Frank to Simon.

'Who's gone?'

'Whoever was here. The lights.'

Simon seemed to hesitate, perhaps as if to imply: was there anyone here? But he too had seen the lights. Leon or Sampson working late? (But in Frank's room?) Some other spy? The real spy? No, Simon was as real as anyone else in Michaelhouse. As unlikely as Bernice or Delaney or Leon or Sampson or Louise, and therefore as likely.

'What do we do?' enquired Frank, although she knew the answer. Not much point in going back now. They might have to go through all of this again tomorrow night. The thought of the smell of the meat, as much as anything else, strengthened her resolve to see it through.

Laboratory Three. Opposite Leon's office. No description—

that was surely significant. The one place that Frank had not been shown over that morning.

This time the first key worked. Simon's thin beam of light slowly circumnavigated the room, up and down. There were no large pieces of equipment. No argon arc furnaces or gamma ray spectroscopes or nuclear accelerators. Just a wooden container twice the size of a shoe box, top open.

Torch searching inside, two heads peering over. Lord Rutherford lives again, Frank thought to herself, at the sight of a mass of little pieces of wire, crossing and criss-crossing in decidedly unaesthetic fashion. There was definitely a rubber band over there, and another, down in this corner.

Two buttons roughly fixed to side of box. Simon Jeffrey, wanting some dividend for his carefully planned break-in, presses one. The green one. Before Frank can think, council caution, try to persuade—before she can even be afraid. One wire moves across to complete a pattern. A small propellor on the front of the box kicks twice, like the real thing, and then whips into life. Faster and faster, the whirr becomes a hum and then a shrill whistle before it is lost to both eye and ear. Frank presses the red button. The moving blade becomes once more visible, losing speed very slowly.

Point made. Pasars—if Frank had doubted it until then, which she probably had, in one corner of her mind. Pasars were for real. Just a few old wires. If you knew to connect them together in the right way, in the correct order, at the appropriate angles. As set out in Pasar papers. Vital pages resting in a safe. In the office next door, belonging to Sir Barry Stone, one to which Frank had not been admitted that morning.

It was large and—even by torch-light—comfortable. Four easy chairs, not as capacious as that in the Master's study, but pretty good for a nine-to-five office. Large blackboard bearing formulae. Leather-topped desk. Blotter, old-fashioned inkwell. Large heavy green curtains, where Frank's office had only a dirty venetian blind.

Simon was already crouched in front of the safe. Wafer of light dissecting the knobs, numbers, inner cusp, outer foil.

'It'll take me about an hour.' And Sir Barry had fondly imagined that if he died the thing would have to be blown open. 'Not as hard as I thought it might be,' Simon added.

'Did Uncle Mose . . . ?' Frank began. She had an image of safe-cracking lessons. The Bradford burglar and his astute but impatient pupil. 'No, no, little Simon, five to the left and four to the right. Now, there's the click, listen!' Mose might spin the knobs again, and invite the youngster: 'Now you do it!'

'No, no, no,' Simon explained. 'I spent a year working between school and university. At Chubb's. Once you know how they're put together it's easy enough to get them open.'

If Simon was going to be crouched over the safe for an hour, how was Frank expected to occupy her time? Keeping watch? But Dr Jeffrey had that planned too. 'You go and look through Leon's room, and Sampson's. The same key should do. And you'll find a spare torch in the bag.'

Frank wanted to ask what exactly Simon expected her to look for. This would have been somewhat in vain because her mentor had now donned a stethoscope and was plainly engrossed in his task. Tap, tap, listen for something. Turn again. Now this dial, now the other.

Well, Frank knew what *she* would like to find, or she thought she did, and that would have to do.

Close the door on Simon, resisting a temptation to lock him in. Sampson's room first. The filing cabinet wasn't even locked. Three copies of his slim thesis, already typed and bound, and dated April of next year. When his scholarship finished? Frank believed in being organised but this did seem a bit extreme. Five files of pencil notes, all in Sampson's handwriting. Rough notes, crossings out. Cryptic titles like 'meta-field', 'linear focus' or just 'regression'. Nothing beginning with P.

She sat for a moment in the single vinyl-covered chair. Simon's success rating thus far was 100 per cent. Assume that he does open safe. Takes out fifty-three vital pages. Puts them in bag, amidst pliers, ladder, spare batteries, streaks of blood.

What then? Should she take them off him, at gunpoint? Tie Dr Jeffrey to a chair and call Lord Johns at the number by which he could be reached twenty-four hours a day? That would safeguard the secret, or what was left of it, but leave unanswered every important question. Like how Simon would get them to the Chinese. Why Most was murdered. Why a stone face had almost flattened two people in Michaelhouse Court. (Or was that really an accident?)

No. Simon would take them home, on his stolen bicycle, accompanied by trusty Frank le Roux, right there at the heart of the crime but without the first idea of what to do. Watch Simon day and night? Ring the security people? Undertake a bit of burglary on her own? Pinch the papers from the thief and observe his reaction?

Leon's office was larger, one armchair, thin browny-coloured curtains. No safe. One filing cabinet, locked. Picture on desk of square-faced lady. Slavic. The wife he had to leave behind? Frank picked it up. The other side bore another picture, of another lady. Same sort of age, softer lips, harder eyes. Be sure to put it back the right way round.

Simon's keys—Uncle Mose's keys—opened the filing cabinet. It all seemed so easy. (Too easy?) File after file. All of Leon's life was in that metal box. Residence permit. Inventory of modest share portfolio. Bill for dress suit. Subscription notice for Cambridge Jazz Appreciation Society.

Second drawer, first file. PP at top right of each page. The word Pasar did not occur, but P . . . ? PP45 began: 'Chain linking of P. units has been shown to yield exponential output. This was confirmed by preliminary experiments to order five.' And the five had been crossed out in pencil, replaced by seven. 'P. applications, although theoretically unlimited, will in practice be restricted by quality of materials and accuracy of assembly of individual P. elements. For practical purposes an optimum will have to be arrived at—between low cost and high efficiency. It is recommended that a range of different grade P. prototypes be tested for suitability in a variety of social and functional contexts.' And so on.

Frank hastily examined the page numbers. PP1–20, PP45–100 and PP184–197. That was all. Frank looked at each piece of paper in every file, an hour and a half's slow scanning. No more bits of Pasar document. Lock up Dr Ivanovitch's office.

Simon was still rapt in his work. His hobby? People usually pay more attention to their hobbies than to regular salaried employment. He looked up as Frank came in, nodded. One finger lifted as if to say: almost there.

Suddenly a dull footstep in the corridor. Heavy, like the steps of Satan—as Frank's mother might have remarked. She shivered. Simon continued—twist, tap, listen, twist, tap, listen. The night watchman moved slowly, inexorably, through the building. No need for a light to open the safe. Touch, feel, sound. The watchman's torch kept a steady passage down the middle of the corridor as he trudged around the building, half-conscientious, half-asleep.

Frank withdrew to her own room. Saw, with a start, message still on board: BEWARE OF DEATH, SHE STRIKES BUT ONCE. That piece of paper handed to her at the Union debate. Was it only last night? Still in Frank's pocket. GO HOME YANK, with a murderous skull-and-crossbones drawn below, in red ink.

Frank carefully compared the handwritings. O and E, letters without character. N, anyone might draw that the same. But H, compare the Hs. A little different. Could they be by the same hand? They could. Differences *might* not be significant. Oh dear, Frank remembered her one course in Statistics. I should have a hundred samples of each style to see whether the Union threatener always makes the left-hand stroke a little longer than the one to the right, and has the cross line extending beyond both verticals. But, on reflection, Frank decided that two hundred threatening letters might be rather too much to take.

Who could have left the message on her board? Leon, Sampson, Stone, Louise—all worked in the Kavendish. Delaney had certainly called. Bernice? Who knows? Would Simon have written on Frank's board and then brought her along as accomplice, sent her off to poke around? Stranger things have been known to happen.

Frank picked up the eraser and firmly wiped out the threatening epigram. Wouldn't do for it to be seen by the cleaners.

Questions might be asked, and attention was what Frank did not require.

Simon, after two hours of checking and elimination, was at last showing emotion. Stethoscope now discarded. 'Four more possibilities,' as he swung the outer knob once more—left, right, left, left again. 'And if they don't work I have to start again. Must have missed something on the inner coil.'

'Find anything?' he asked as he himself drew another blank.

'Like what?'

'Well, you know,' Simon expostulated, certainly giving the impression that he didn't. 'Files marked secret. Anything like that?'

'No,' Frank was relieved to be able to answer truthfully.

The safe door swung open. Even gave a squeak as if it wasn't used to such exertion. Two flashlights plumbed the mat black interior. Frank looking for fifty-three pages of patent Pasar puzzle, Simon searching for what only he knew.

But surely not for a bottle of whisky, Haig, half-full, and three-quarters of a packet of McVitie's chocolate digestive biscuits. For that was the precise contents of Sir Barry Stone's most valued safe.

'Where have they gone?' Frank's cry was involuntary.

'What?'

'Oh—er—the secrets!' After all the burglary team had come with certain expectations.

Simon seemed totally lacking in surprise. 'It just shows,' he advised, 'these scientists are just laying down a yarn. They bull themselves up as God almighty, spend millions of the taxpayers' money, and what is there to show for it?'

The last words were lost in a gulp as Simon lifted the whisky bottle to his lips, gurgled, wiped them. At least he didn't drop dead. Frank took a biscuit, bit it, hoped Sir Barry didn't keep them counted. Then she suddenly realised that it was hungry work, negotiating electric fences and huge dogs and rifling through files.

There was no secret message on a thin slip of paper secreted in the middle of the biscuit. And there were lots of things about this case which just didn't make any sense at all.

VII

Sleep, for Frank that night, was just preceded by the touch of head on pillow. Five hours of fulfilling slumber broken only by a dream in which Andrew Delaney, captain of a paddle steamer on the Mississippi, forced first Simon Jeffrey and then Ms Frank le Roux to walk the plank, right into the jaws of waiting alligators.

No good waking with a shiver, there was work to do. Saturday breakfast—of all times—was the weekly meeting of Michaelhouse Fellows. Eight am, for an hour or a bit more, Bernice had taken pains to explain at dinner the previous night. Frank would have to take her breakfast with the students, apologies for forcing such a fate on their honoured guest.

Bernice would be there, and Barry Stone, Leon, Simon Jeffrey, Andrew Delaney; and Sampson Ndagbera was a Research Fellow. Yes, he was expected to attend. And did.

Time for a bit of burglary on her own account. Frank didn't have Simon's mass of equipment but it was amazing what a piece of twisted wire could do on the heavy but primitive locks in the second oldest college of the second oldest university in England.

Sampson's room wasn't even locked. Tidy, like his office, and little sign of its owner's character or interests. Only college pictures. Record player—Beethoven, Mozart, Vivaldi. And under the mattress—how sweet, Frank declared to herself—under the mattress were Pasar pages one to a hundred, precisely. Jot numbers down in notebook. Leon's office at the Kav had yielded PP1–20, 45–100 and 184–197. That still left over a hundred pages unaccounted for.

The next room she tried was locked. How could anyone like Leon Ivanovitch, fresh from the Soviet regime, do otherwise? As untidy as Sampson's was neat. Piles of clothes on the chairs, on sofa, mixed up with physics textbooks and jazz magazines. Frank spent half an hour looking around, mostly in unlikely places. Not a single Pasar note.

Time should, most definitely, be watched. Surely today, of all days, the meeting would not finish before nine. Simon Jeffrey's lock took three minutes to unpick. All the gyps, Frank had observed on Friday, were required to serve breakfast in hall.

No time for a careful investigation of Dr Jeffrey's abode. Just look in the likely places, predicted from what she'd observed of his Jekyll-and-Hyde personality. Now where might Uncle Mose have recommended as a good hiding place?

Frank's nail file was handy for unscrewing the wooden panel holding electric radiator in position over ancient stone fireplace. Well, the screws had plainly been undone recently, crumbs of paint on the rug. Simple. Simon had placed a large manilla envelope straight on the old grate—not even pushed out of sight up the chimney. One envelope containing eight pages, PP1–8, slightly blurry photocopies but still quite readable.

Thought was not permitted until Frank had regained her own room, locked that door most securely, donned tights, tuned in to danceable music. A French station! Wonderful place, Europe, the whole world seemed to be around one, all there in the radio receiver. It was almost claustrophobic to someone used to North America, or Australia. Or China?

Who was Simon Jeffrey? What was his role? Broad-tongued, cricket-loving hobbyist burglar—breaking into the Kavendish just because it was there? That was the façade, and a most persuasive one. Why then did he have eight Pasar pages hidden in his fireplace? Had he only got the first eight pages? In that case he still had a long way to go. But the Chinese already had some of them, according to Lord Johns' agents. Were those Simon's own file copies? Surely, if he *were* a spy, he wouldn't be that stupid.

Second question. Frank tried to stretch her mind in time with limbs. Gyrating to Franglais rock, unfolding, extending, a dance of release and also of purpose. Why on earth had Simon taken her along with him? Sure, company is good, especially on a long midnight errand. But spies act alone. They have to. It's the first rule of the game.

The radio started a spitting tirade of French political opinion. Plenty more stations. Cool German swing, body moving easily and smoothly, warmth returning. Frank's thoughts turned to those fifty-three Pasar pages. They wouldn't be noticed as missing until Monday morning, if then. How often did Barry Stone open that famous safe? Whenever he felt like a slug of Scotch, or had the old Australian craving for a bikkie?

If vital papers had been removed from the safe it was a most serious matter, and Frank should surely inform someone. Stone? Lord Johns? If someone other than Simon had taken them then Simon wasn't the spy. But what of PP1–8 behind Dr Jeffrey's fire?

What was the light doing on in those three Kavendish offices at 11.30 last night? Had *that* been the spy? Another spy?

Perhaps Sir Barry Stone, who was certainly no fool, didn't keep civilisation-changing secrets in obvious places like the safe in his office. What about a bank vault? Why should he have told Frank the truth? Well, she reflected, it was after all said at the moment of truth.

But couldn't Stone himself be the spy? Perhaps he'd taken those pages off to photocopy or microfilm over the weekend.

Breakfast in a coffee shop next to Laura Ashley's. Two thick black mugs and one French pastry. People streamed past. Country folk, come into town for Saturday shopping. For the first time since Frank had arrived the pale earnest students and haughty dons seemed outnumbered, lost in the crowd of perfectly ordinary gossipy down-to-earth English people. Pale faces, worsted trousers and faded gingham dresses.

It was nice just to wander around Cambridge. Down past Caius College, then the Senate House. All the gargoyles hereabouts looked secure enough. Through Clare College. Clare garden, just over the Cam, had been recommended by Delaney. 'Open to visitors in the afternoon, Monday to Friday only.' That would keep most genuine visitors out. Well, perhaps if they hadn't that rule it wouldn't be here at all. Frank vaulted over the low gate. No barbed wire, no 24,000 volts, no hungry Alsatians. Just a scented walk among tulips, daffodils, grass which looked as if every blade had been individually cut, cut with a razor.

The Modern Languages Building on Sidgwick Avenue—a definite destination. Some architect who had wanted to spend as much money as possible, for the minimum of actual working area; the whole building raised up on pillars, ground floor high in the air. But the library was still open. There was just one thing Frank needed to know, and it shouldn't take a minute to check.

Heffer's main bookstore, right across the road from Michaelhouse, had a line of people twenty yards long. What, all for an omnibus edition of the works of Plato?

It turned out, as Frank pushed her way into the shop, that the demand was for something slightly more salacious. Dr Bernice Dodds, newly coiffured and wearing a most revealing blue dress, sat in the window autographing copies of the new enlarged edition of *Primitive Procreation*, smiling at each prospective reader—who all seemed to be men over thirty or women under twenty-five, Frank noticed with her practised sociologist's eye. Inscribed with what sentiment? Did Bernice size up their height and build and proclivities and recommend for each the most appropriate position?

Two large tables piled with this garish production. Surrealistic yellow and red cover that could be interpreted as two speckled pigeons building a nest, as sunset over Hawaii, or—with a bit of rabid imagination—as Chinese and Red Indian having it off in a swamp. Frank leafed through a copy. A possible present for her brother in Memphis?

Chapter Three, section Four, 'Fluvial consummation'. Amongst the Pranto people, Frank read, a prince must always achieve first union with his wife in the river, at least three hands breadth from the bank, standing vertically. Bernice then noted the peculiar soapy nature of rivers in Prantoland. Really! Who's to know if she didn't make the whole thing up? Well, her bank manager wouldn't care, that's for certain.

Leon Ivanovitch, just behind the mêlée, appeared to be absorbed in a paperback biography of Kim Philby. Engrossed.

Frank had to tap him on the shoulder to attract attention. Leon snapped the volume shut, covering title with hand, although there was a pile of copies on the table before him. Maybe that's the way people do react after living among the KGB for most of their lives? Frank gave him the benefit of the doubt.

'Well, what have you been doing, Frank? Find out anything at the Kavendish?'

It must be lack of sleep. Frank's instinctive thought was: how does he know? But to Leon the haunted look that momentarily darkened her face was probably a familiar sight.

'Yesterday morning,' Frank had to remind herself. 'Yes, it was a start. But a study like this takes time, you know. To build up a picture of how people do interact. Can I interview you—on Monday morning, say?'

'Certainly,' said in a voice which implied that *she* would be doing *him* the favour. 'But I could tell you quite simply now. Anyone who wishes to talk with me, I talk. If they are involved in their own work, I keep away. My door is never locked, you might say. I am at all times—how is it said?—attainable.'

'Available,' Frank corrected.

'Yes, quite. And now I have a proposition to put to you.' Leon projected a pleasant anticipation. 'How would you like to accompany me to London on Tuesday? I have to visit Grosvenor Square, your American Embassy, and I must see some scientific colleagues at University College. Come,' he invited, 'and you shall see me interact with them!'

Great stuff, Frank's mind went into overdrive—but what's the real reason, for chrissake? Will he feel happier going to our Embassy with an American? Oh, what the heck!

'Sure, I'd love to come, Leon. You can show me some of the ancient sights.'

'I am so glad.' Her hand was grasped between two large freckled Slavic paws, perhaps a bit like being thanked by a grizzly bear.

Saturday lunch was just buffet in the combination room, Leon apologised. The gyps were given the afternoon off, to go to the races at Newmarket or whatever. Poor dons, Frank commiserated, having to actually put food on to their own plates because the servants were permitted a single half-holiday per week.

Leon removed silver covers from chafing dishes that crouched over low gas flames. Pity our poor board! Our poor groaning board. Trout stuffed with pine nuts. Beef and lobster. Avocado salad. Frank saw that his eyes did light up, a remembrance of the exigencies of food shopping in Moscow; a gleam of joy protruding through the blasé front that Leon had assumed, chameleon-like, in his new life.

'I suppose we did do right,' he sighed.

'Did do what right?' Frank asked, as she was intended to.

'Well, with all this inflation the college investments don't yield as much as they used to. Last year we had a sort of financial crisis. It was necessary to vote on whether to reduce the standard of food for the Fellows, or just have one less Fellow.'

'And you chose the second alternative,' Frank presumed. She didn't see how the food could be any better.

'Yes. I voted against it.' Leon used a toothpick to dislodge a stray strand of lobster. 'But now I repent. One cannot allow standards to be corroded.'

'Eroded, you mean?' Frank wondered, to be answered with a nod.

Other fellows were now partaking of the makeshift repast. Bernice—cool, totally unruffled by having autographed some hundreds of copies of her off-white Kama Sutra—put her plate down opposite Leon. Frank noticed that she did, however, attack the trout entirely with fork held in left hand.

'By the way, Frank,' Bernice recollected. 'Someone was looking for you. Superintendent Selvey, from London.' She took a mouthful of lettuce and, mostly, avocado. 'In connection with the Master's murder, you know.' The sweetness of Bernice's smile, as she said this, vied with the rather definite stress she placed on 'murder', making the first vowel long and deep and sinister. Did he actually have the handcuffs out, Frank wondered about asking.

'Yes, he was here talking to all of us.' Barry Stone had sat down next to Frank, his knee coming up against hers, momentarily, reassuringly. 'He asked if he could see you on Monday afternoon at two.'

'Just before the funeral,' added Bernice, in such a tone that Frank imagined she might be thrown into the grave with Most's remains—to be buried alive according to some ancient Cambridge custom—if the Superintendent's worst fears were realised.

'He couldn't stay around this afternoon, had to go off to Newmarket,' continued Sir Barry. It wasn't clear whether it was the Superintendent's afternoon off too, or if he were to investigate some high-level doping conspiracy. Still, Frank felt a little cheered. If it had been anything other than routine, the man from Scotland Yard would presumably have stuck around for another hour or so to see her.

Leon and Bernice became engrossed in discussion of the Michaelhouse May Ball, swapping opinions with Delaney and Simon Jeffrey about the relative merits of bands and champagnes. This allowed Sir Barry to enquire—indirectly, but quite effectively—about the success so far of Frank's mission.

'Get any clues yet about the kind of factor that might inhibit my lab from operating to maximum advantage?' That established a sufficiently euphemistic level of communication.

'Could be anything. I've never met a trickier situation,' Frank raised her eyebrows and shrugged the one hand that wasn't concerned with eating.

'But you must have some lead, some hypothesis?' Sir Barry found it hard not to fall back on scientists' jargon.

'Like trying to catch minnows with a wide-gauge shrimp net,' Frank told him. 'You get something in sight, then it's through and away. Have you any ideas? Is everything all right?' Even if they'd been alone she wouldn't have wanted to say: Are those vital pages still in your safe? I know they're not, because I helped Simon Jeffrey to penetrate your impenetrable fortress, about ten hours ago.

'Pretty well. But I do have one dark suspicion.' Sir Barry slightly tilted his head towards Sampson Ndagbera who was staring indecisively at what was left for lunch on the hot plates.

He was about the only one Frank hadn't seriously suspected.

'You must tell me about it.'

'Monday morning,' Sir Barry agreed. And dinner with Sampson on Monday evening should give a bit more of an insight into how that brilliant but inscrutable mind ticked, Frank reflected as she was called to answer the telephone.

Lord Johns. A trifle impatient. Any progress? Well, Frank put on an authoritative, confident manner that belied an inner emptiness, she had a number of leads which were being followed up, day and night. All the suspects were being systematically checked, their holdings of parts of the Pasar document noted . . .

'You'll recognise it by PP and a number at the top right corner. Oh, and the word "Pasar" doesn't occur—just P.' Lord Johns' voice was brutally businesslike.

'Yes, that accords with my own observations.' Frank was perfectly able to put on the same act.

'When we spoke on Wednesday, pages one to eight had been traced to China,' he continued. In China and on the grate behind Simon Jeffrey's electric fire, Frank grasped the receiver a little more tightly.

'Now,' continued the voice of government, 'we have information that pages nine to twenty have followed them.' A pause to let that sink in. 'And it appears that they are getting into China through Taiwan, of all places!'

Frank le Roux didn't seem quite as mystified by this extra piece of news as Lord Johns had perhaps expected. Slightly the reverse, although she didn't show it. The Prime Minister, Frank was told, had twice enquired what progress was being made. That lady expected results.

She shall have them. 'Give me three more days,' Frank tried not to sound pleading. She had chosen the longest time that she thought might be acceptable to Her Majesty's Government. Ask for three weeks and they'd have bundled her back to New Orleans on the next plane. But three days? Frank's main ambition was to live that long, even if she didn't manage to locate the leak.

VIII

'YOU COMING FRANK?'

She had been eating strawberry cheesecake. Eating it mechanically, her mind on little bits of wire at carefully controlled angles that could generate immense power. Sir Barry Stone had gone home to cut the lawns, he'd informed Frank without euphemism.

'Simon's decided he'd like an afternoon on the river too. That makes four of us so we'll take two punts.'

She had never seen Andrew Delaney so organised or animated, as they reached the tiny square of grass which was all Michaelhouse owned of river-front. 'How about Grantchester, then? We can show Frank the old church and have a cream tea.'

There were just two punts locked up by the wall. One had stained brown wood with orange cushions, just like the other punts that passed back and forth along the river, students relaxing after tripos, tourists not quite sure what to do but enjoying it for all that, and an occasional load of yokel youths, sullen in their unease.

The other punt, into which Simon Jeffrey immediately stepped, was quite shocking. Pink. Painted bright pink all over, inside and out, pink pole and pink cushions.

'Jump in, Frank! This'll suit your colour scheme.'

Frank looked ruefully at her pink blouse, red corduroy slacks, red sandals. Andrew and Sampson seemed to be fully occupied working out how to unlock the brown punt. Well, if the local Johnsonian expert can safely get me in and out of the Kavendish he should surely be permitted to punt me down the Cam, decided Frank, as she lay back on pink cushions and looked up at the grey stone façade of Michaelhouse.

Delaney was in charge on the other punt, pushing off from the bank as Sampson Ndagbera worked his knees into a comfortable position. White ferries black, if only our great-grandfathers could have seen this day. Then such thoughts were back-grounded as Frank noticed a face move away from a third-floor casement on the nearest Michaelhouse wing. A familiar face? Just a face. Unrecognisable, but one that had definitely been watching the departure of Professor Delaney's afternoon boating expedition. Now who lived on that staircase? Would it be K, or L?

Psssugh! Bang! Attention riveted on St John's. A punt just by the Bridge of Sighs. Falling projectile. White object. Lands in middle of punt. Screams from passengers. Water flying everywhere. Those are not the frantic, frightened cries of people injured, or are they? No blood mingled with the dirty river water.

'Silly buggers!' Simon half-apologised for childish prank perpetrated by students from another college. 'Just a water bomb, that's all.'

'What's that?' asked Frank, at the risk of appearing foolish.

'A paper bag full of water, I think. Aim it properly and you have a bunch of very wet lady tourists. Make their day, I expect—to be water-bombed by a *real* Cambridge undergraduate.' Just for the last sentence Simon's Yorkshire accent reappeared, as if he were mimicking what Mrs Tourist would tell her mates back in the Barnsley Mothers' Union.

Having reverted to the voice of his origins Simon continued in the same vein for punting lesson, part one. 'I'll go down to King's bridge, and then you take over. You'd better watch what I do carefully, Frank.'

It didn't seem very different to Frank from helping her father shift contraband in large, open shallow-draft boats. Punt a little, paddle a bit, across the quiet bayous in those steamy moonlit Louisiana nights. Punt-poles were pretty good for menacing any cheeky alligator that threatened to slide under the boat and upset its balance.

Another water-bomb from the no doubt bow-tied joker in St John's. He always did it to ladies? Delighted screams and arms could be seen all akimbo as Simon moved them swiftly around the bend. Now gliding past the Wren library at Trinity. Best not to say anything nice about the architecture of a neighbouring college. It might turn out that Josiah Wentworth had a brother who could knock Christopher Wren into a cocked hat, only all his buildings fell down through no fault of his.

'Ah, the twenty-eighth of May,' sighed Simon, as he dug pole into river bed, pushed hard, with a deft final twist to set course for the exact centre of Trinity bridge.

Today's date, Frank said to herself. So what? I'm damned if I'll play stooge to every single don in Michaelhouse.

'That's the day I finished my book on Rasselas,' Simon explained, as if she had asked. 'At 11.32 am the final *t* was crossed.'

'Why did you write yet another book on Rasselas?' Frank felt obliged to contribute something to the conversation.

'Yes, that's why. There aren't very many of them, you see. It was my PhD thesis, and it was time I had a book out, you know, so the Press said they'd publish this. But it had to be revised a good deal.'

Clare College garden from the river. A different view, different combinations of colour—bright yellow, mellow blue, chattering scarlet. Dr Jeffrey was writing history. His own. 'I suppose in the next century people will write PhDs on my book, just as I write about Johnson. Comparing the original thesis with the published book, deciding why I altered this and changed my opinion on that.'

I doubt it, I very much doubt it, mused Frank. 'How long did it take you? Isn't Johnson supposed to have written Rasselas in one week, just in the evenings? To raise money for his wife's funeral?'

'Ah yes, well, he *was* a genius,' Simon allowed. 'My final draft was started at 9.35 am on the fourth of February last year. Precisely 478 days, 117 minutes for the whole task. Come on, it's your turn now.'

Frank walked carefully down the middle of the punt to take hold of the pole Simon proffered. So Simon wanted his place in history, did he? Writing books on Rasselas was probably *not* the way to ensure it. Stealing the secret of a fantastic new energy principle might well be the right way.

What was it they said about spies? There were three possible motives. Love of some country or cause. Hatred of ditto, and a desire to betray. Or just the need of money. Frank now added a fourth: yearning for fame. Mata Hari and Simon Jeffrey—yes, no doubt at all, that would look rather fine in the history books.

Punting, Frank found, wasn't quite as easy as it looked. Particularly if one were trying to psychoanalyse Uncle Mose's nephew at the same time. The pole, for a start, was rather heavy. And its centre of balance seemed erratic. She threw the pink pole up all right but caught it with hands too low so that the top veered over, out of control, and missed Dr Jeffrey's head by about three inches.

'You're doing fine,' he encouraged as Frank tried again. This time stuck the end right down, pushed as hard as she could—must need special muscles for this, like cycling—and then found it was so tight in a bunch of weeds that a last frantic jerk was of no avail. One pink punt moving upstream and pink pole wavering against the bank, five yards off.

Andrew Delaney might have been following for just such an eventuality. Sampson grabbed Frank's pole as they came alongside and then chivalrously reversed his hold as he held it out to Frank, top end towards her. Like handing someone a knife.

'Hey Simon,' Delaney called across, 'Sampson was just telling me he thinks Barry Stone should be the next Master. I told him can you imagine Lady S. as Master's wife? I ask you, a plumber!'

So, Most didn't have any wife at all, what's the difference? Frank decided not to worry her head with Cambridge ranks and what you should or shouldn't do. Her main aim in life just then was successfully to negotiate one pink punt under the mathematical bridge. Just pieces of wood at the correct angles, no nails or screws. Rather like Project Pasar? She saw Andrew Delaney squinting at that crossing place. Same thought, perhaps.

Then Silver Street bridge. A big push, against the current, or they'd get only half way and start floating back. Pull pole over to right at end of stroke. Hell—that was the wrong way. Simon had out the emergency paddle to push against a brick wall into which the Michaelhouse pink punt was heading, and then negotiate them out into the pond by The Mill.

People were sitting at a table in front of that pub, dressed in pressed creams, brighter dresses than any Englishwoman would wear, under a gay umbrella. Drinking Foster's Lager for the benefit of an energetic film crew. Advert for Australian television?

'Keep to the right,' Delaney instructed the novice punter, 'away from the lock. There's quite a current across that side. We'll take them over the rollers. Just follow me!'

Which Frank actually did. Simon jumped out and three Michaelhouse Fellows pulled the punts, one at a time, up a steep bank of metal rollers on to the upper river beyond the lock. Let them do it, Frank decided, temporarily suspending her ideals of equality.

She then let Simon punt her upstream. Past expensive hotel and then out of Cambridge. Meadows with incurious sheep. Tracks across the flat marshes leading to ornate iron footbridges under which Dr Simon Jeffrey, that paradoxical, monomaniacal, littérateur-cum-burglar, punted with assurance.

'"Here the sons and daughters of Abysinnia lived only to know the soft vicissitudes of pleasure and repose, attended by all that were skilful to delight, and gratified with whatever the senses can enjoy."' The second youngest Fellow of the second oldest college declaimed Dr Johnson's novel as they seemed to float through the East Anglian countryside.

'"They wandered in gardens of fragrance and slept in the fortresses of security. Every art was practised to make them pleased with their own condition."'

Frank le Roux, Saturday afternoon and all that, ought to have relaxed. Did try to relax. Surely there was no sharpshooter behind that tree, or crouching among the cows. Her bag, with a small jewelled revolver, was one tiny piece of insurance. Lucky she hadn't had it along when John Fisher descended almost on their heads. The squashed contents of that bag had been solemnly handed her by the Michaelhouse porter. One mirror in ten thousand pieces. One address book, the paper now like onion skin. One bunch of keys, slightly twisted. A flattened revolver might have caused comment.

But in fact that 'accident' had suggested to Frank that self-defence might well be needed. The silence, as Simon punted into Grantchester, was broken only by small, dark-coloured English birds. Like the womenfolk, they didn't go in for bright colours. But the other silence, the absence of any violent accident or threatening letter since the DEATH message on her Kavendish blackboard at 5 pm yesterday—that was distinctly ominous. Some person or persons wanted Ms Frank le Roux to stop what she was doing. She hadn't. Would they?

Simon Jeffrey had brought along the pink punt padlock. Delaney hadn't. But they could just about tie the two up together. Or at least make them *look* as if they were secured.

Walk across the meadow to Grantchester. Some nice old buildings—but not really as 'historical' as lots of Pennsylvania. Cream teas. Line of people about a hundred yards long. No wonder the English have a word 'queue'—they need it, Frank thought.

'I was telling Sampson he ought to think about Fermat's Last Theorem,' Andrew announced. Simon betrayed no surprise. Probably everyone around Delaney knew about $a^n = b^n + c^n$ where n is 3 or more. 'He'd be able to prove it. Stand a very good chance, anyway.'

Untoward modesty wasn't one of Ndagbera's characteristics. He didn't deny he might be able to provide a proof. Just: 'I can't see what good that would do for my h'people, Andrew.'

'What good is all that work you're doing over at the Kavendish?' demanded Simon. Consummate actor, pretending that he didn't know the marvels of Pasars? Or didn't he know? For goodness sake, Frank told herself, *we* saw it *together* last night. He pressed the button. He *must* have known what that was.

'Everyone ought spend at least six months of their life working on Fermat's Last Theorem,' Delaney declaimed. Then he added, with finality: 'You can't call yourself a mathematician if you haven't.'

'Perhaps the ju-ju man wouldn't approve.' Simon's taunt

appeared all the worse delivered in his broadest Yorkshire. But that presumably was what he intended—mock racism, an in-group joke between friends.

Sampson Ndagbera was—there was only one word for it, as far as Frank was concerned—a gentleman. But also one with common sense, and humour. 'I'd get out my ju-ju mask and hex you with it, foreign scum,' his eyes twinkled, 'if there wasn't a h'woman present.'

'Jujus don't like h'women,' as an added explanation.

'Chauvinistic devils,' Frank interjected.

'Oh, they're definitely devils,' Sampson agreed. 'And aren't all devils chauvinistic?'

The queue had just snaked inside the garden. Leaving the two Englishmen to wait their turn and obtain cream teas for four, Sampson and Frank claimed the only spare table.

'It's a nice life here,' Frank ventured.

'Too nice. People get to like it too much, then they never h'want to move,' Sampson replied. 'They are supposed to be the clever people, the leaders, but they don't spare a thought for the h'rest of their country. Unemployment, inflation, all that. Or for the rest of the h'world. Like Nero playing his violin while Rome burned down around him.'

Them's strong words, Frank reflected. From the man Sir Barry Stone had hinted might be the mole, if one wanted to employ proper espionage terminology. Sampson was certainly a most determined person. But there were many open questions. Why didn't he just submit his PhD and go home now? If anyone could reconstruct Pasar theory back in Nigeria Sampson could. Did he permit himself just three years of carefree paradise, the length of his scholarship? And why had Sampson fainted at the Feast last Wednesday night? Why did no one bat an eye when he did?

Four plates arrived. Hardish scones, a dollop of cream on each, and a speck of strawberry jam. Teabags in tepid water in four cups.

'One pound twenty-five each for this bit of junk,' Simon complained. 'Lucky Leon isn't here. He'd tell them how much the raw materials cost and what the profit percentage is.'

'Leon'll be going off to the States soon,' Andrew observed, as if it were as inevitable as the first cuckoo.

'Yes, I asked him to stay in h'Cambridge this summer,' Sampson reported. 'Because of the h'field theory we are working on. But he h'can't. He has to teach in a summer school. In h'California.'

'Why don't you go along too?' Simon enquired.

'What, and miss all the German girls coming to Cambridge to improve their h'English!' It was hard to know whether or not Sampson was joking. Maybe a bit of both.

'Leon should go and live in America, he's there so much.' This sounded like a complaint from Simon.

'He did try to, didn't you know?' Andrew fastidiously licked cream from each finger in turn, and then started on the other hand, although that hadn't in fact been near his tea. 'When Leon left Russia he had a good job offered at Cornell. But he couldn't get a visa and came here instead.'

'If he couldn't get a visa, how come he goes there every summer?' Frank felt impelled to defend the policies of her country by drawing attention to this inconsistency.

'Oh he gets a temporary visa all right,' Andrew explained. 'But the difficulty was with a permanent residence visa. I'm told it was because he'd been a member of the Communist Party. The US immigration officials wanted Leon to sign a statement saying that he'd been forced to join the party against his will. And he refused. He was prepared to admit in retrospect that joining the party had been an error of judgement, he said, but he had *not* been forced to join. It had been of his own free will.'

'Honest chap,' Simon declared, to a hearty nod of approval from Sampson.

'So no declaration, no visa,' Andrew concluded, 'and America's loss was our gain.'

'But he's settled here now?' Frank enquired. 'He seems happy enough.'

'One imagines so,' Delaney agreed. 'All that was some years ago. Come on, time to show Frank the church.'

Which, as churches go, was nothing really special, Frank

privately decided. Old, yes. A few bits of stained glass. But no real character. Rupert Brooke's poems could have been even better if he'd been able to gather inspiration in a building that had more resonance, mellowness, tone.

A sign to 'Byron's pool'. The imagination boggled, what had he done there?

'Come on, time to go back. My turn for Frank, I think.' Thus spake Andrew Delaney who was after all organiser of the afternoon. He talks as if I'm some chattel or, at the opposite extreme, a queen. Frank settled for the second alternative.

Delaney's punt was the brown one. Just as well, the shining pink had been beginning to engender a headache. Frank took the pole as Andrew tried not to show surprise, or annoyance. 'Go upstream a bit further!' he directed, determined to have some say in things.

Then, settling back on cushions, elbows spread, hands behind head, one knee in the air and the other leg at right angles, heel resting on said knee: 'Wonderful things, punts. Do some of my best research on the river.'

'Is that all?' Frank now considered herself quite skilful at punting. Throw the pole up, push it in at ten degrees to the vertical, right against the side of the punt, push back pulling against boat if direction needed to be changed to the right, or moving the end of the pole around the bow for the other direction. Punting was getting almost mechanical, so that attention could be directed on to Professor Andrew Delaney, absent-minded when it suited him, someone who was in a position to know all about Project Pasar. And to pass it on?

'The things one can do in a punt are quite unlimited,' Andrew assured her. 'With a bit of skill. Although not everyone is able to find a quiet bit of river like this.'

Or a quieter-still backwater, Frank thought, as she steered the boat just out of sight. Better to be safe than embarrassed. Why on earth do I bother with these bourgeois white middle-class susceptibilities? But I do, she sighed inwardly as she jammed the pole in as deep as possible to secure their craft against the bank. Delaney tied the painter to an overhanging branch while looking at Frank, returning gaze—direct, acquisitive, expectant.

Words were not something Delaney depended on heavily. Nor Frank. Gestures. Tactile, kissing, gently pressing. Divesting oneself of garments. No urgent hurry. Movements can be graceful, fluid, broken by osculation. Frank to Delaney. His hands, lips, tongue on her breast. Moan, around and about, sinuous bodily oscillation.

Odd noise, scraping, lapping. Realisation only when wave cascades over entwined bodies that they are in a punt. That this was the original point of the suggestion. 'Better get dead centre,' the posh professorial accents reduced to no more than a vocal creak.

Two can play at being scientific. 'The centre of gravity should be as low as possible,' as she cajoled him into position and then rose, deftly, inundating senses with feeling, smothering thoughts, suspicions, jealousies. The Professor of Pure Mathematics became a primal being—hands and lips, striving and grasping, psyches enfolding, gently blending. Bodies coaxing and being coaxed. If the wires are at the correct angles they shall generate power, Pasar power. Limbs crossed and entwined. Pushing, searching, striving, floating—suspended in mid-air, to hover, glide, dive and then ascend in a wave, a crescendo of power and passion and florid fulfilment.

A small red-backed bird squatted on the branch, pecked at the painter.

'Nice to get away from all the hassle of Cambridge,' Frank finally ventured.

'Yes, I suppose you have had a rather calamitous time.' Delaney kissed one ear, neck, right along arm. 'What with deadly nightshade and falling masonry. And all you wanted was to study how people get on in the lab.'

Frank traced her finger along Delaney's ascetic back. 'I've only spent one day in the Kavendish but there's something I can't put my finger on. Something that doesn't seem exactly right. Is there some fabulous secret, do you know Andy?'

'Well there is this Pasar stuff. That's a huge secret.'

It was like being at school with someone who told you: 'hey, have you heard about so-and-so but don't tell anyone because it's an absolute secret,' and you say yes, of course you wouldn't breathe it to anyone, but in fact someone else had told you half an hour before with the same proviso.

'What's Pasars?' Frank kissed, sucked at her captured professor's left lobe, which required no effort at all, but pretended innocence, which did.

'Sorry, I shouldn't have said anything. Wipe it from your mind!' Delaney commanded, and then explained: 'It's a gadget that Barry Stone and Leon think will give cheap power or something. Not my field at all. I'm a pure mathematician, you know.'

Are the compartments that watertight? Or if they are, then surely you're also a human being, concerned about what's happening in the world. Frank ran her fingers through his hair, hoping it felt as good to him as Andrew's doing it did to her. Tingly. Why not come straight to the point? 'What if someone stole the secret. Who'd do that, do you think?'

'Who'd want to do that, Frankie?' The thought seemed genuinely not to have occurred to Delaney as he adroitly swung around. Enough talking. A jerk at the painter made red-backed bird retreat, for safety's sake. Now dipping, rising, slow gentle fusion of mind and temper and bones and flesh. Fuller, richer feeling. More confident, more serene. More biting, engulfing, entrancing. One blond American girl, calls herself black. One just-middle-aged Cambridge don. Two people. Boat responding, side to side. Water shipped on to feet, oddly uncomfortable. Forgotten in tumult. Bells, drums, gongs, bombs exploding, cohering, building—a high tower to the sky. Pinnacles of flame and life. Two cries mingled together like the scream of a crow.

They lay in the bottom of the brown punt without talking. And then Andrew Delaney made to get up.

Sure, why shouldn't it be his turn to punt. Need to get back for dinner. Never forget mealtimes at Cambridge, the fulcra of existence.

There was just one topic that worried Frank. Slightly nagged at her, in an odd way. 'The Mastership thing is of great sociological interest, you know Andy. Who would you fancy for it?'

'Hard question that. I rather think an outsider would be good for the college. Lord Johns might take it. But I'd be just a bit worried about his morals, if you know what I mean.'

Frank didn't. Might he seduce the undergraduates? Female or male? It became apparent, though, that Delaney was using the term in a wider sense. 'You know how Philby and Maclean and Co. were up here in the thirties, when there was a lot of sympathy for the Russians?'

She nodded.

'That's all well-known now—but it was kept hidden for decades.' Delaney was moving the punt along at what he would call 'a lick'. With the current, back into fields of sheep and cows and magnificent butterflies. 'What isn't as well known is that there was a big pro-China group here in the early fifties. When Lord Johns was up. He actually joined the Communist Party—it took me a while to uncover that. So maybe if he was that open he is okay now,' Delaney mused.

'But Lord Johns is Head of the Home Office,' Frank couldn't help expostulating.

'I know,' Delaney gloomily agreed, as if most of Her Majesty's Ministers were ex-communists, potential spies.

'Would he want the Mastership?' Frank persisted. 'Would *you* want it, if it were offered you?'

'Oh yes, of course.' Delaney's impatience with this question didn't seem to leave open the possibility of asking 'why?' But, Frank pondered as she took over the pole in the interests of continued equality, simply—why? Would I have to be an anthropologist to uncover—or, more important—to understand the reason?

'Did you ever get married?' Delaney enquired, as he lay with evident pleasure, watching Frank punt, head tossed back at the end of each stroke to lollop hair out of eyes.

'Well yes. I still am, in theory. To an Englishman.' Which is why I sometimes come out with funny English idioms, Frank decided against adding. After all, no one would think them unusual here!

'He's called Johnny,' she added. The connection of names didn't elicit the glimmer of a smile from the contented professor. It would for Leon, Frank thought, he'd know that song. 'How about you?'

'Oh, yes, yes.' Delaney seemed rather vague about the whole matter, flinging one arm out in the direction of the west. 'She's at Oxford now. Likes it there. Punts from the wrong end of the boat, you know.' As if that were sufficient sin to justify eternal damnation. Frank wanted to ask if she'd come back and be Mrs Master should Delaney land the job everyone yearned for, but it somehow didn't seem quite appropriate.

The rollers were easy in reverse. Just keep the punt straight and gravity did the rest. Let Delaney now guide them home. Frank's arms were feeling tired, numb. The Australian film crew were still at it in front of The Mill, actors now a little sweaty and looking quite sozzled after four hours of Foster's Lager. Take forty-seven, clap.

'I thought you'd have been in favour of Lord Johns as Master if he had communist sympathies, Andy. On with the revolution, that sort of thing.'

Delaney steered them expertly under the very middle of Silver Street bridge. One long push, crouch down, and ready to shove pole right down as soon as the stone canopy was cleared.

There was only a touch of impatience in his voice. 'Surely you know that the revolution won't come about if we have fellow-travellers in top jobs. It must start from the bottom. The more we can get reactionary leaders, real right-wing conservatives at the helm—that's the best recipe for a real revolution, a workers' revolution.'

'Anyway, it was thirty years ago that Lord Johns belonged to the party,' Frank proffered. 'Just a youthful fling perhaps. He seems the very pillar of respectability now.'

'Quite,' agreed Delaney. 'Silly to say he might be a spy.'

Andrew Delaney seemed to be lost in thought, looking over towards Queens' new buildings. Frank's mind needed to be kept very clear. No one had suggested that Lord Johns was a spy. There hadn't been a hint of it. And tie that to the China connection in the fifties . . .

Now Delaney himself was a distinct possibility to be the Pasar thief. But if he was, would he hint at an accusation against Lord Johns, thereby giving away that there *was* a spy, a China-directed spy? Was it an absent-minded slip? Or was Delaney, the only Englishman at all involved in Project Pasar, really patriotic and reliable. And did he know that there was a leak? How—who could have told him? The only people who did know were Stone, probably Patrick Most, and Lord Johns. Frank felt as if she had been mugged—head dull and dopey, brain moving too slowly to sort out the puzzle of Pasars. If it was a puzzle—a solvable puzzle—and not just one huge mess.

Two people sitting on the grassy bank in front of King's—the college with the chapel that was *still* used for religious services—seemed to be waving in their general direction. Frank looked around—there were no other punts nearby. Delaney suddenly took his attention away from punt-pole moving through water, switched thoughts from Fermat's Last Theorem. A large expansive upper-class fling of the arm, too grand a gesture to be simply called a wave. Slightly fatuous comment: 'Hello there. Enjoying the sun?'

Now Frank was able to place them. Roger, the freckle-faced drop-out apple-seller. Woodenly holding hands with Deirdre, slightly down-at-heel secretary who didn't get on with her boss. Delaney's Encounter Group. How sweet that they were getting friendly. Isn't that what people often expected from groups like that—some sort of romantic involvement. Life really isn't like that—the best things aren't premeditated. Except that sometimes, unexpectedly, it may come true.

'Playing the regular tourist guide, aren't we?' It was hard to pick up vocal nuances from a shout, half of it lost in the dirty Cam water. Half mocking? Part congratulatory? Any bit jealous?

'How much do you charge?' Roger continued.

'I am without price,' was Delaney's pitched reply.

King's bridge. Delaney ready to throw up the pole as soon as they had passed under. Does throw it up. Professorial hands out to catch. Remain empty. Split-second shock, realisation, shout, as two townies on the bridge struggle with the heavy wooden rod. Delaney lunges for the end. 'You bastards!' a whip-crack response, long-drawn, haughty *aaa*. If words could kill.

But the pimple-faced youths tighten their hold, now leaning over the bridge as Delaney fights for control, twisting, pulling to extricate the pole from their grasp. Frank gets up, resolutely to take her place on the side of the establishment, lends strength to Delaney's long-armed heave. Finally, right will out. The Michaelhouse pole is once more under Delaney's sole control. Two youths disappear. They've had their fun, made their gesture—probably didn't expect, or really want, to win. Delaney continues undisturbed, as if absolutely nothing had happened.

Frank, from her position on the cushions, has a clear view back down the river. Under the bridge. Roger and Deirdre are doubled up with laughter. Roger, in particular, is laughing like the proverbial drain, as Frank's erstwhile English spouse had been apt to say, describing himself in relation to the police. Odd? A little.

A slight breeze ripples the water. Goose-pimples Frank's arm. Delaney carefully waits until a good two yards beyond Clare bridge before daring to throw up the pole. Same at Trinity bridge. Then they tie the punt up by the tiny Michaelhouse lawn. Delaney solemnly shakes Frank's hand, thanks her for a 'super afternoon'. Disappears inside to dress for dinner.

A bit inconclusive, was Frank's verdict. Things, if anything, now seemed more complicated than before. Delaney? He either did know nothing, or else Professor Andrew was the coolest character Frank had ever met. His room really cried out for inspection. A thorough going-over, tapping for cavities in the wall, loose floorboards, hollowed-out family Bibles (or perhaps copies of *Das Kapital* in this instance). But when? During dinner? Frank was acculturated enough to really look forward to Michaelhouse meals, and it would look distinctly odd if she were absent this evening. Churlish, after the afternoon's entertainment.

Under the Bridge of Sighs—St John's' grand Venetian arch, intended perhaps to make up for the dirtiness of the water—punts could be seen coming and going. One pink punt, unmistakable. They must have gone on up the river, to Magdalene bridge or beyond. Tow-headed Simon Jeffrey at the controls. Sampson must be lying out flat in the bottom of the boat. Draught of hedonism before he returned to refurbish Nigeria, paserise its industry, agriculture, irrigation.

A water-bomb exploded in the distance as Simon ducked under the bridge, waved to Frank. Had that St John's joker been at it for four hours? Happy screams of outraged delight. T-shirts peeled off, hung out to dry.

Nearer, from the jutting angle of Michaelhouse, a faint squeak as a window was pushed open above Frank's head. A hand appeared. Balanced. Aimed. Dropped a large round white object. Another water-bomb, Michaelhouse student imitating his richer neighbours? Not a water-bomb. Too heavy, falls too fast.

Simon Jeffrey pushes pink pole away with fear on face, jumps out of punt, takes one tremendous leap towards the further bank. Bomb falls, right into the shocking pink punt. A gigantic explosion that seems to rock the Bridge of Sighs. Ancient buildings tremble. Shock wave streams Frank le Roux's blond hair behind as she gazes, transfixed, at the disintegrating punt. Then flings herself to the grass. Pieces of pink wood are blasted twenty, thirty, fifty feet. Pieces of pink wood and pieces of Sampson Ndagbera, asleep at the end of a drowsy afternoon. Mathematical genius, the power behind Pasars, murdered in a very efficient if somewhat messy manner. By one powerful bomb, straight into his stomach. Sleep—Sampson Ndagbera will now sleep on.

IX

DINNER WAS SERVED at Michaelhouse High Table that night, but an hour late. There was little talk. Superintendent Selvey had returned from Newmarket to investigate 'before the crime becomes cold', as he put it.

Simon Jeffrey was badly shocked, had been put to bed by Bernice with a stiff sleeping draught. Frank was a prime witness. Well, at least no one could accuse her of dropping the bomb, in the way that Sir Barry Stone had whispered she had had the best opportunity of poisoning Dr Most's chaliced toast. Very careful description of what the bomb had looked like, how it had fallen. Even the hand that dropped it—no cuff had been visible. The superintendent tapped his cassette recorder in admiration—probably the modern equivalent of licking the end of a pencil. 'Social scientist, eh?' he remarked. 'Good observer.'

Frank hadn't done it. And Simon Jeffrey couldn't have been responsible. Although maybe he did have his claim to fame: 'At 6.22 pm on 28th May I was punting the finest *natural* mathematician since Euler when he was blown into a thousand pieces.'

That was the hardest part. The pieces. Well over a hundred bits of Sampson, of his clothing, and of the book he had taken along to read, were recovered. Floating in the water. Sunk to river bed, to be retrieved by large policemen with high gum boots and powerful searchlights. Or thrown on to the banks. They would have to be pieced together, the superintendent explained, for identification. Was that necessary? Established procedures must at all times be observed.

Sampson wasn't a candidate for the Mastership, that was certain. Were all these murders and near-misses connected? Most and Delaney and Sampson—they all knew about Pasars. Which *was* a secret, despite the ease with which all the principals confided in Frank. No, take that back—it hadn't been all that easy. Her techniques were—she liked to think—unusual, and unusually effective. But there were also those two threatening notes, which had been directed at Frank and at no one else.

Little to do that night. No one relevant lived on staircase K or L, that much was easy to check. The Fellows went off alone, to their rooms. To think or read. Or pray? An excellent idea, if that sort of thing took your fancy.

Frank explored. Found a discothèque. Tiny, tucked away. No one who looked like students or dons. Loud, enveloping music. Forgot about energy and investigation and small bits of black skin. Pretended she was a sales girl in Laura Ashley, or Woolworths. Saturday night out. Let body out, to play and swing. Rhythm, happy cavorting dance. No mind to call one's own, not on Saturday night.

And on Sunday morning, sleep late, helped by dull sky outside, heavy clouds as if the sun had died with Sampson Ndagbera. Which it had, in a rather real way, for mathematics, for Nigeria. But at least his genius had yielded those Pasar equations. Unlimited power for the world, including the third world. If, that is, it didn't become unlimited destruction.

Which church to attend? Not, it must hastily be added, that Frank was a deist. She'd have agreed with Karl Marx and her father, for rather different reasons, about the function of religion, and didn't herself feel the need for an escape clause in life. Who made the world? Frank didn't know. And to those who thought they did she wouldn't bother to ask 'Who made God?'. Every person to their own rationalisation, their own scheme of life. Just as long as they didn't try to force it on others. (Which, unfortunately, a number of Christians and Moslems do, and perhaps other sects as well. Although missionary work does have its good points—how else would Sampson Ndagbera have learned to read? One of the questions Frank would have liked to ask was whether Sampson actually believed in a God. The Igbo type or the Christian variety? Or both? Or a blend of the two? It was too late now.)

King's College Chapel. There really was no other possible

alternative. For the atmosphere, which was what Frank savoured most. Anyway, it might not be used for religious services much longer, if Professor Andrew Delaney had his way.

Frank le Roux was still registered for the PhD dissertation on socio-economic parameters affecting urban church-going. And she did still take notes, each Sunday, into a large, stiff-backed notebook that went along on all her missions.

But most of all a church was a place for Frank to resolve things. Straight thinking, putting personalities and plots and motives in order, that she did at night to music, mind purposefully dancing along with body. It was solving the conundrums, actually getting the flash of inspiration that cut to the core of a case—more often that not the idea of a solution came in a church. Any sect, Frank tended to choose a different denomination every Sunday.

It was hard to tell what role Frank's mother played in her obsession with church-going. Certainly her mother beamed a contented smile when Frank was able to answer 'yes' to enquiries about regular attendance at places of worship. Frank had many times explained that she went as a sociologist—as observer and not as participant. And that it was a different variety of shrine each week—Methodist, Moslem, Baptist, Buddhist, Orthodox or Anglican. 'At least you're there,' was the reply, 'and He knows you're there.' Frank had never confided about churches and temples being a great place to get ideas, solutions. She knew exactly what the maternal comment on that would have been.

Those little choir boys in their big top hats. Like something out of Dickens except that they did look reasonably well fed. Frank had a seat at the front, under the elaborate wooden screen that had been carved for Anne Boleyn. Mind wandered away from woodwork. Who had wanted to murder Sampson? *Had* they intended that Sampson should be the victim of that unwater-bomb?

A shiver, like a spasm. Right in the middle of a hymn. *Immortal, invisible, God only wise.* Someone had watched the punts depart. From a window in Michaelhouse. Was it the same window as that from which the bomb had been dropped? Frank couldn't be sure. She should have paid more attention. The same, or else one close by.

That face had watched two punts depart. One a shocking pink with Simon Jeffrey punting and Frank le Roux—inquisitive, elusive visitor—as passenger. The pink punt had returned with Dr Jeffrey again at the helm, a passenger lying asleep, face perhaps covered by book or handkerchief. That passenger had been bombed, despatched into the next life (if perchance there should be another) in more than a hundred small pieces.

Frank le Roux could have been poisoned, after only a few hours in Cambridge. She could have been squashed flat by that large ancient masonry head. And she could have been eliminated from this world by a bomb.

Let us pray! Never had those words been spoken at a more appropriate moment. Frank sank down gratefully, knees on to cushion. Buried head in two slim hands. Let him say his Our Father, his Apostles' Creed or whatever formulaic incantation has to be directed at the local deity, in order to see the people of Cambridge through another week. Let me see my way out of this damn mess. I don't have any Pasar secret. Why kill me? Because I might find out something? Fat chance of that, Frank told herself, as the congregation rearranged itself on benches to give at least partial attention to the sermon.

Maybe I'm being paranoid. And a bit megalomaniac. Frank tried to think rationally, never a very easy thing when one is frightened. Most, Delaney, Sampson—why weren't they the intended victims? Two of them did die. All knew about Pasars. Maybe the killer will strike next at Sir Barry Stone, director of the whole project, or at Dr Leon Ivanovitch, émigré genius. Was he really loyal to Britain? Having lost one patriotism had he so easily embraced another? Perhaps Leon was sending the secrets back to Russia. He could be the killer. Or Stone. Or Delaney—perfectly possibly, and John Fisher could have fallen spontaneously. Or Louise. Don't discount Louise. Who was it had called her a 'cute cookie'? She was clever—by that interpretation it was surely an accurate description. Why had she stopped

Delaney on Thursday night in the Union? Had he been about to allude too loudly to the Pasar work. Damn, Frank chastised herself, I should have asked Andrew what else he had planned to say.

The moral, as Mister Preacher wound up, seemed to be that you shouldn't steal. Good message, Frank decided, but just at that time she'd have preferred a somewhat stronger one. Don't kill, for instance.

More preoccupied, more muddled than when she'd entered, Frank was really in no humour to be accosted by Louise. 'Wasn't that a wonderful service! Good music just makes one feel closer to God, don't you think? Isn't it just awful what's happened at Michaelhouse this week?'

It was odd how someone who was not normally effusive could suddenly become effusively sad. Frank didn't want to explain that she didn't go to church to be nearer to God, whoever or whatever he or she was (if anything). She did feel sad, for more reasons than Louise knew, but didn't feel at all like talking about it, which only made things worse. But she did have a job to do, a job in which you couldn't take Sundays off since the other side didn't. And Louise was certainly a piece in the puzzle.

'What on earth's happening at Michaelhouse? Have you any idea, Frank? Is there some homicidal maniac in the college? I can tell you, I locked my window last night. And put a chair against the door.'

And if you had any Pasar pages I should have left them outside the door, Frank refrained from suggesting. What she said was: 'There must be a reason. There's always a reason. Sexual jealousy, that's why most crimes are committed, you know. Or money. Or some secret, something which would fetch a fair dollop of dough.'

Louise didn't seem to have listened to any of this. 'Who would have wanted to kill Sampson? He was such a good man. Polite, considerate. I can tell you, some of our Blacks in the States could take a leaf out of his book.'

Thanks a lot, Frank saved up for some later occasion. 'Is there any secret around Michaelhouse that someone might be absolutely desperate for?' she persisted, adding, to make things perfectly clear: 'Or in the Kavendish?'

'Oh gosh no,' Louise hesitated. 'I don't think so. Well—' she stopped. 'I mean no one would actually kill for a secret, would they?'

'Of course they would. To keep a secret or to get one. I'm sure that every day someone is killed for one of those reasons, in some part of the world,' Frank stated. 'So why not here? Especially if some foreign country is involved. Political ideals. Or, as I said before, simply money. The green stuff.'

'Oh no, that's ridiculous. You've been reading too many thrillers, or Hollywood films about conspiracies and things.'

Or actually been a participant in them, Frank grimly reminded herself. She should just press Louise one more time. A reaction that didn't seem really genuine, even when you stripped away the Ivy League front (surely just as affected as Delaney's, in its own way). Why did Louise deny so vehemently the slightest possibility of Most and Sampson's murders being connected with Project Pasar? When she had *some* knowledge of what was going on, Barry Stone had been sure of that.

'Look, Louise, surely it's *possible* that the murders could be connected with some awful secret that outsiders want?'

'Absolutely not,' the first all-American, all-female President of the Cambridge Union insisted. 'It must have been because of sexual jealousy, like you said.'

By which stage they had reached Michaelhouse. Just in nice time for Frank to decline a glass of sherry before Sunday lunch. Fellows still grim-faced, Superintendent Selvey invited to join them for traditional fare: roast beef, Yorkshire pudding, potatoes, sprouts. It tasted like roast rump—if beef could ever melt in one's mouth!

Leon was the only person who still had a twinkle in his eye, even an occasional smile across those mottled Slavic lips. 'This is a terrible homicide. And the most brilliant student in the whole of Cambridge. We were to work on field theory together. Now I will have to go it solitary.'

'Alone,' Frank corrected. Big grief now, but you weren't prepared to forgo a trip to the States for a summer with Sampson on field theory. Maybe I'm being uncharitable though, she decided. Leon and Sampson would have had the whole of the next academic year for that project.

'Would you accompany me to the Cambridge Jazz Club tonight, Miss le Roux?' Why the sudden formality, she wondered. 'Ken Colyer's band, from London. He spent some time in New Orleans about 1950, jumped ship in Houston, do you know the story?'

Frank didn't. But that would surely make him almost as old as some of the veterans who played Preservation Hall. Although not as good, she'd be bound. 'Sorry Leon but I hope you understand, I wouldn't really feel like going to a jazz club today, not after what's happened.'

Leon quite understood, or said he did. Not everyone found his habit of drowning grief in laughter totally congenial, he remarked, although that seemed something of a misstatement. Frank at least didn't make a habit of laughing at jazz bands.

Lord Johns—when eventually the ever-available number gave another that turned out in fact to be Ten Downing Street—remarked rather peremptorily that he'd been expecting Frank to ring. Rather earlier in the day, it seemed to be quite clearly implied. First Most had been murdered—well Lord Johns was there for that, he could hardly hold Frank responsible for not somehow preventing it. And now someone who did matter, 'that African chap'.

Frank didn't like to say that whoever it was might have been trying to bump her off. Perhaps Lord Johns would prefer that he had. At least he'd still have Sampson alive and the whole case could just be turned over to Superintendent Selvey.

The Prime Minister, Frank learnt, was extremely concerned. Her relations with the rest of the Commonwealth might be sullied, for one thing. But at least Lord Johns didn't mention that any more Pasar pages had been reported from China. Maybe there was still time for something to be done.

When eventually he ran out of steam Frank was able to say a little about her activities. Just enough to mollify. Monday would be spent in Cambridge, mostly at the Kavendish, and helping the good superintendent 'with his enquiries'. For Tuesday she had promised to accompany Leon to London.

Aha, confided his Lordship, the Prime Minister would probably want to have a few minutes with Frank. For a personal report. Sure, Frank realised, that's exactly when my three days run out.

There was just one request Frank had. Not too difficult to organise. Lord Johns agreed without, luckily, requiring too much in the way of explanation. Well, at least it showed that he still trusted her. It was nice that the British *were* reliable and dependable, Frank decided. And that might well be the most important thing of all.

That afternoon Frank spent in her armchair reading *The Masters*, which really explained a lot about what was happening at Michaelhouse. With the door locked. Then evensong at Michaelhouse Chapel—well, even a visitor must show a jot or two of college loyalty. A packet of fish and chips from a most un-university place on King Street, smuggled into the Arts Cinema. *Last Year in Marienbad*, what a film for the relaxation of Frank le Roux, private investigator, stymied detective (unless that flash of an idea an hour earlier . . . might really be . . . ?). Baroque, allusive, timeless, the movie could well have been set in Michaelhouse. With Bernice Dodds as the heroine? Either her or Frank le Roux.

Monday morning the sun shone again. Reflected in the gleaming body of Sir Barry Stone's Porsche, nine o'clock on the dot. No further mention of Frank getting a bicycle.

As Senior Fellow Sir Barry had been busy in Michaelhouse all Sunday. The Nigerian High Commissioner had come up in person. There were telephone calls to Igboland, to mathematician friends Sampson had made during his two short years in England. The funeral service arranged for Monday afternoon, for Dr Patrick Most, would now include Sampson Ndagbera as well. Probably he'd be known as Dr Sampson Ndagbera. The PhD thesis could be submitted, and the degree awarded posthumously. That was surely the least they could do.

It was odd to drive in through those three Kavendish fences. Tall one, peaked with barbed wire, gate just standing open. The electrified fence, current switched off between nine and five, a guard who raised the boom at the first sight of that shiny Porsche. Then the third, smaller fence, gate also open. A growl from off right, clank of metallic leash, indicated that the Alsatian was well recovered from its drugged sleep.

And the Pasar papers? The only thing actually missing from the Kavendish would be those crucial pages from Sir Barry's safe.

'Let me know what I can do, Frank,' as he waved her towards an armchair. 'We need action quickly I'd say, after recent events.'

'You think that Sampson's murder was connected with the Pasar leak?'

'What else?'

'Look, Barry. You did hint on Saturday that you thought Sampson might *be* the leak, didn't you?'

The Director winced. Never speak—or think—ill of the dead. But social susceptibilities have to be backgrounded when a crime has been committed. A whole series of crimes.

Frank hadn't really thought that one through before. No time like the present, while Sir Barry emptied the contents of his briefcase, made three neat piles of papers on the desk. Sampson could have written that message on her board. Plenty of time in the morning, while she was at Sir Barry's boring meeting about chain idlers and suchlike. And he could well have been responsible for the note passed to her in the Union. As for poisoning Patrick Most—and perhaps trying to poison Frank as well—Sampson had recovered from his faint at just the right moment. He must have passed that golden chalice while returning from the combination room.

'Back last Thursday morning,' Frank reminded him. She did not need to specify exactly where. 'You thought Patrick Most might have been the spy. Then you said Sampson.'

'Most was a guess,' Stone admitted. 'I just couldn't think that anyone on Project Pasar could be a traitor. But Sampson had been behaving a bit strangely. And there were odd things like someone had been making illicit photocopies, not entered on the log. Someone with a key to the Pasar rooms.'

Probably just Leon making copies of articles on some obscure jazz musicians, Frank thought. 'None of the critical Pasar pages have gone missing, have they Barry?'

'No, they couldn't have. No one else knows the combination.' He responded to her silence by looking up, meeting Frank's gaze, her brow slightly furrowed. 'You want me to check?'

'Wouldn't do any harm.'

'No, I suppose not,' he agreed doubtfully. Sir Barry Stone knelt in front of the safe, extracted a thin sheet of paper from his wallet, twiddled knobs, quicker than Simon Jeffrey had, no stethoscope.

Three minutes, by Frank's watch. The thick gun-metal door swung open. One half-empty bottle of Haig whisky. Part of a packet of biscuits. Those Sir Barry ignored. He lifted a thick envelope from the bottom shelf, held it gingerly, balanced on four fingers of right hand, as if the slightest jerk might prove fatal. Slipped pages from envelope on to his desk. Wet one finger, quickly skimmed through page numbers on top right-hand corner.

'Pages 131–183. They're all here,' he announced with definite relief. And finality.

There was nothing more to say. To the Director everything was as it should be. Frank could scarcely blurt out: but they weren't there at two a.m. on Saturday morning. Someone took them out of your special safe. Made copies. Put them back. A microfilm may even now be on its way to China. (Via Taiwan, of all places.)

Sir Barry had another ten o'clock meeting. And Frank should get on with her sociological study. Or pretend to. 'You must come round and meet my wife some time, Frank. I'm sure you'd enjoy each other—have a lot in common.' Oh yes, the plumber. Well I hope she's better at dealing with leaks than me, was the inane thought that came into Frank's head as she set off down the corridor.

Just for the cover, an hour chatting to the glassy metal boffins. It might not be totally irrelevant. What did an outsider think of Project Pasar? Of Leon and Sampson and Stone, not to mention Delaney. And I mustn't forget Louise, Frank issued a self-reminder. Behind that glittering exterior . . .

Paul Todd, chief protector of the argon arc furnace, was co-operation itself. He estimated how many hours each week were spent on working alone, working with others in the research team, on seminars, on administrative tasks. Which colleagues were forthcoming, which reticent. 'It takes all types,' he explained. 'Some people get an idea and have to talk about it at once. For others this would be impossible. They must work it out, articulate every detail, be able to answer every type of question before daring to share it.'

What interaction was there between research groups? With Sir Barry's project for instance? For the first time their conversation became strained. Sir Barry, apparently, was not operating within any accepted theory of physics. He'd done good work in the past, Dr Todd allowed, but now . . . ? Incipient senility? All this vague talk about a new kind of energy source. It was like the alchemists three hundred years ago, trying to turn lead into gold.

It appeared that the glassy metals people didn't have any contact at all with Project Pasar, didn't even know the name of Barry's breakthrough. Well they did in a way—it was jokingly referred to, when important backs were turned, as Stone's Folly. Maybe Sir Barry had purposely organised things that way, maybe it suited him.

But there was one thing, Todd hastened to add before taking Frank off for morning coffee. That fellow, hick Australian he might be, off-beam physicist, whatever else you might say: 'He's a brilliant administrator. Looks after us all. Makes sure we have everything we need for our own research. He really has a knack of getting money.'

Frank decided against spilling Sir Barry's secret. He just spends as much as possible (within reason, of course) and they give!

The conversation she then had with Leon was singularly inconclusive. He was helpful but not forthcoming, Frank decided. As he'd told her before, the Ivanovitch door was always open. How much of the week did he spend on this and that and the other? 'I do not know. I have no watch. What does time matter? How much time do you spend in the toilet? Or making love? Of what consequence is it?'

Where were you at midnight on Friday night, Frank wanted to ask. Did you look out of staircase K at two pm on Saturday? What do you know about explosives, or poisons, or levering large blocks of stone off slightly crumbling pillars? Instead Frank apologised for taking up so much of Leon's time.

'I would rather talk,' he insisted. 'Work is impossible. My grief is too distraught. My student, my friend, he is no more. Lost, vanquished for ever.'

Vanished. Frank forbore to offer the correction. It wouldn't anyway be strictly true—not until those hundred pieces of corpse met with the hot flames of the crematorium, in a few hours' time.

More time to talk with Leon tomorrow, away from the office. Sir Barry was going off to play squash. 'Must keep fit, you know, especially at my age,' delivered with a broad Australian wink. Frank preferred to walk back to Michaelhouse. Noisy roar of traffic along the main road from Bedford and Northampton. Then Wilberforce Road, its quietness punctuated every thirty yards by a patient driving-school instructor—invariably male, fortyish, bestubbled—putting a nervous beginner—female, twenty-five, mousy hair—through a succession of three-point turns.

Superintendent Selvey—at the two pm appointment made before ever Sampson Ndagbera had been blown to bits—was courteous but firm. He'd already taken down Frank's impression of the fatal bomb. Now it was back to Dr Most—seemed like five months in the past, not five days.

Barry Stone's inexorable logic might have appealed to Selvey, had he been in possession of all the facts. Frank carefully said that she *had* just drunk from the chalice before Hervey de

Stanton decided that life wasn't all it was made out to be stuck up on a wall. So there was only Most left to drink—and everyone at the Feast knew that.

It wasn't all that fair, Frank admitted to herself, deceiving a fellow-worker. If she'd said that she hadn't had a chance to sip the toast it would have made clear to Selvey that the target could have been Frank or Most or both. But he would also have seen that only Frank could have ensured that just Most died, by making sure that none of the liquid went past her own lips. The idea of being arrested, or taken down to New Scotland Yard for questioning . . . ! Of having to ring Lord Johns, get the Prime Minister out of bed! She might as well just catch the next plane back to New Orleans.

The superintendent was coming along to the funeral. In the tiny chapel of St Michael. Maybe he hoped that the policemen's patron saint would flash down a sudden bolt of inspiration.

It was a sobering occasion. Funerals always made Frank sad even when she scarcely knew the person. Dark suits and ties in the hot May sunshine. Andrew Delaney, again honourary tourist guide, pointed out mathematicians from Oxford, Salford, York, Warwick, Nottingham and Imperial College London. Most, on the other hand, seemed to be mourned by one person—albeit one rather formidable person, Bernice Dodds, grief merged with guile as the Mastership elections loomed closer. The day after tomorrow. The day after the May Ball.

Superintendent Selvey went along to the crematorium, cassette recorder now put away in pocket, jotting occasionally in a notebook. Where he goes, I go. Frank stood next to Leon as first one polished oak cask, and then the other, slid off into oblivion. 'Ashes to ashes, dust to dust,' the great Russian physicist whispered, perhaps hoping it would remind Frank of home, 'if the whisky don't get you, the women must!'

Monday night. That had been when Sampson had invited her out to dinner. Wonder what sort of meal he'd have gone for? Chinese? Indian? Or British to the core?

Well, no time for sentiment. Death's angel was surely still stalking those ancient staircases—St Michael or no St

Michael—and Frank's main ambition was to cheat him of his next victim.

Andrew Delaney ate his dinner, announced that he was going off to the ABC. Sit in the front row, like Wittgenstein used to, and let the modern-day equivalent of cowboys and Indians blot out the world. Frank didn't like to add that Wittgenstein never—absolutely never—ate at High Table. He'd pick up a pie on the way, to munch in the movies.

That did leave the coast clear for a most careful examination of Professor Delaney's abode. Everything so neatly arranged that great care must be taken to leave no sign of intrusion. One drawer full of white shirts. The one below had different shades of blue, carefully arranged in a gradation of hue from darkest to lightest. Books in alphabetical order. Blotter on desk exactly parallel to sides, pencils laid against it, head to tail, head to tail.

Nothing. No Pasar pages. No concealed interstices in which anything could be hidden. Just one locked drawer in the desk. Any key would do. A sheaf of letters, neatly clipped together. They told of love. Unrequited love, from brief perusal probably unrequested love. Each was signed 'Dodger'. Funny!

What's sauce for the goose is sauce for the gander, as Frank's mother had used sometimes to comment on her high school daughter's chagrin at the isolated times when a boy actually turned down her invitation to a Prom. Quite. But still Frank was rather taken aback to find that her own room had been ransacked. Totally—no subtlety, no attempt at disguise. Drawers emptied on to the bed. And Frank's fat notebook, notes for the probably-never-to-be-completed dissertation. Left open at the last page, two paragraphs on the kind of townspeople who attended Matins at King's College Chapel. Below a simple message, written with Frank's own pen. In block capitals: GET OUT!

X

Dr Leon Ivanovitch, apart from that thick accent and the occasional choice of a word, was now more British than the British. Deep in *The Times*, as the train pulled away from the longest railway platform in the world. Under the Hills Road bridge. Past plushy new offices and printing plant of Cambridge University Press.

Minute study of factional disputes in the Labour Party, in the Conservative Party. Astute references to Disraeli. Letters from retired Generals about the poor standard of toilet facilities at Victoria Station. From retired Admirals about sporting links with South Africa. Stock Market report—keep the stags at bay. Leon grinned or scowled, nodded and tut-tutted at the minutiae of British life. The only thing he didn't study with the true deliberation that would have marked a born-Britisher was the cricket scores: 'Boycott achieves new batting record.' But that might come, give him a year or two more.

Frank had bought the tabloid *Daily Mirror*, as a counterweight. Found it almost completely devoid of content. Okay for picture of brazenly buxom but probably empty-headed bus conductress from Birmingham. Big spread about twins reunited after forty-odd years, who found they had fillings in exactly the same teeth.

'Is there any foreign news in your paper, Leon? Anything on the crisis in the Far East?'

A grunt in return. Dr Ivanovitch was being singularly uncommunicative. Maybe he wasn't at his best early in the morning. Head now stuck down, mouth screwed up over *The Times* crossword puzzle. He merely passed over to Frank the middle part of the paper, so that she could search out for herself information on who might have assassinated the Emperor of Japan.

Eight different extremist groups had claimed that doubtful honour, Frank read. 'Hey, Leon, there's an interesting article here. Did you know they've eliminated VD from China?'

This did elicit some response. 'How?'

'Medical cure, of course, but mostly just changing the whole community's attitude towards sex. It says that all Chinese now regard it as a responsible act, not just a whim of joy.'

'Pah!' Leon's expostulation would surely have been worthy of the editor of *The Times* himself. 'That country must be the most boring on earth. I hate China.' The virulence of this expression quite startled Frank. 'It must be worse even than Russia.'

'Yes,' Frank half-heartedly acquiesced, 'I suppose the fact that you can't get married till you're twenty-five, and then can't have more than two children . . .'

'I have five children,' Leon announced.

Some comment was required. Frank knew that Leon's wife was still in Moscow, had not been permitted to leave with him. And he surely would not be allowed to send back money to support his family. 'And your wife still manages to work?' she wondered.

'I have two wives.' Leon's intonation did not suggest that he was describing anything in the least unusual. 'They both work, of course. Katrina, who bore my two sons, she is a computer programmer. Sonya, she has my three daughters and is a dentist.'

'You couldn't marry them both officially?' Frank felt rather lost, or somehow naïve.

'Of course not.' These explanations did not interrupt Leon's systematic completion of the crossword. Four down, ten letters, C-A-N-T-E-L-O-U-P-E. 'Sonya is my wife in the eyes of the State. But Katrina equally in my eyes.'

The train stopped, briefly, at Harlow. Frank's mind still felt numb. Of all people! There were lots of questions she'd have liked to have asked. Did he spend half the week with each? Who got four days and who three? Or a week each, turn and turn about? Did the wives get together and swap stories about what a difficult husband Leon was? Gang up on him? Do they see each other now that he's gone? Do the children play together? Can Katrina's sons have the Ivanovitch name? It must be the sociologist in me, Frank wondered. No—just simple primeval human curiosity.

Leon was still engrossed in the crossword. But he was also warming up to the day, getting ready to communicate a bit more. Which involved—as a first measure—seeking Frank's help with his half-completed puzzle. 'Twelve across. Seven letters, the third one E. "This type of horse is within a long-sighted glass and without a spherical plaything." Spherical plaything must be "ball" and a horse without balls is a gelding. Seven letters. But that does not have E in the right place. And I cannot understand "long-sighted glass".'

'Oh look, Leon,' Frank protested, 'I'm terrible at crosswords. My mind just doesn't work in the right way.'

'I do them because they help with my English,' Earl Ivanovitch replied. 'If I wish to become a native, it is the most I can do.'

'Least,' Frank suggested.

'Yes the least,' Leon agreed, 'but also the most, surely. What could be a greater effort?'

Most. Dr Patrick Most, recently deceased, murdered. Frank wondered if any Pasar pages had been among the Master's papers. That information would have been one gain from telling Superintendent Selvey just who she was—the most unlikely detective in the most unlikely job—and pooling resources. But Lord Johns, when the question was put over the phone on Sunday, had said: No, definitely not. Why? Was the superintendent not reliable? (Was Lord Johns not reliable?)

And the Mastership elections would come up tomorrow afternoon.

'Leon, one thing I can't understand is the Mastership of Michaelhouse College.'

'What about it?'

'Every single person would give their right arm for it. What for? Would you take the job if it were offered to you?'

The paper was now put away, folded neatly in Leon's briefcase, crossword perhaps to be completed on the return journey. 'Most assuredly. It would be the greatest honour possible for me. But I stand no chance, they tolerate me only. I would never be promulgated, in this old class-ridden society.'

Promoted, Frank presumed he meant, but didn't like to offer corrections too often. And she was busy trying to make some sort of coherent picture out of Leon's medley of opinions. Did he mean he actually approved of the class system in Britain? Russia had something similar within the party hierarchy and he hadn't cared for that, had he? The only really classless society was surely China, the object of Leon's scorn. Or was that a front?

They passed in and out of tunnels, through the eastern suburbs of London, windows level with the railway track, washing on the line getting dirtier and dirtier in the smoke.

Leon Ivanovitch had finer opportunities for getting at Pasar papers than anyone except Barry Stone. Almost one hundred pages lay there in his filing cabinet. But they didn't include pages 131–183, of which there was supposedly only one copy, locked in Stone's safe. Except on Saturday night. Still, Leon was no fool. If he had stolen the vital pages they surely wouldn't have been left around for Frank le Roux to find.

'Here we are,' as the train jolted to a halt. 'The Embassy first. Then I take you for lunch. And in the afternoon some shopping and visiting colleagues.' There was one other quite tentative item on Leon's mental agenda that he thought it better not to allude to in advance.

Liverpool Street Station, Frank decided, was just about the most depressing place on earth. Dirt, noise. Long staircases and corridors. Everywhere as far away as it was possible to put it. They followed signs to the Tube station (cute name for a subway system). Surely a great circle route? Didn't we pass through this nexus of rank underground passages ten minutes ago?

'Leon!' An urgent whisper as Frank pulled him against the wall just around a corner, barely managed to avoid putting her foot in a small pile of dogshit.

'What is it?' His tone indicated: I'm supposed to be in charge, what are you doing?

'That man in the grey raincoat and trilby hat. He's been following us. I'm sure. We took a wrong turn back there, must have, and came along here twice. So did he.'

Leon, rising immediately to the situation, slowly extruded his head around the corner. The gabardined gentleman was simply leaning against a wall, reading a newspaper. *The Times*, in fact. Waiting—for what?—half-way along an ill-lit rank-smelling tunnel.

'He must have seen us stop.' Frank pretended to berate herself for acting like an amateur. 'He must have seen me looking around at him, and then grabbing your arm. Come on, quickly!'

The Central Line, to Bond Street, nearest station to the US Embassy. Leon made as if to protest, and then simply shrugged his shoulders as he was led on to the opposite platform, eastbound trains to Woodford and Epping. They walked down, stopped opposite the opening which led across to the westbound platform. A dozen other people entered. Trilby hat sauntered along, the merest glance in their direction. Attention riveted—yes, on the crossword. Pen out to actually fill the thing in.

Train came in, going all the way to Epping. Every single person got on except Leon, likely to be late for his appointment, and Frank, who was here to be shown round London. One raincoated man, now sitting on a bench, was scarcely noticeable. Train departed. The platform filled up again. A party of Dutch tourists, shorts and rucksacks, milled around the space between pursuer and pursued.

Distant roar from the tunnel. No, not this platform. The train could be heard to stop. Frank suddenly grabbed a fat Slavic hand, jerked, ran lightly through and just on to the westbound train as doors shut, held them open for Leon, shut again as Trilby hat could be seen pushing between fair-headed Hollanders, five seconds too late.

'Why?' Leon demanded. 'Why would anyone want to follow me? In Russia, yes, in my last months the KGB they are everywhere. But that is the past. Who would do that here? I have done nothing.'

Frank shrugged her shoulders. Funny he never considered

that *I* might be the object of attention, she noted. But if Leon had been trailed by the KGB for years, it really was understandable.

People at the Embassy were kindness itself. A bit surprised to see Frank, soft New Orleans lilt, apparently waiting for a visa for her own country. But Leon was greeted like an old friend. 'Which part are you planning to visit this time, Dr Ivanovitch? Santa Barbara! Great place. I gotta cousin there. You look him up. Carlo sells insurance. Sure, you'd have a lot in common. It's all figures, I guess.'

There was a lull while the thick black book was taken in to the Consul. The fact that Leon had been a communist necessitated approval from on high, for the issue of even a visitor's visa. The crossword was unearthed. 'Twelve across. "This type of horse is within a long-sighted glass and without a spherical plaything",' Leon mused. 'What can that be Frank? Seven letters. Something-something-E-something-something . . .'

'I'm damned if I'll tell him,' she resolved. 'Leon, did you ever have any difficulty getting a visa? I mean, the first time, after you'd just left Russia?'

'No, none at all.' The answer seemed a trifle peremptory.

Just then a smiling assistant came up with the visaed passport, to be met by an equally broad freckled grin from Leon. 'Have a happy day!' A phrase surely as empty nowadays as 'Good morning'—said even when it is raining—and 'Goodbye'—which many people don't know used to mean 'God be with you.'

'Come, we have time before lunch to look over the latest jazz releases.' Leon steered her to the south, through Berkeley Square.

He doesn't suppose that I might prefer something different. Like wandering around that Salvador Dali exhibition at the Royal Academy. But Frank allowed herself to be led into Green Park Station. If today's task was to observe Dr Ivanovitch, then he should certainly be allowed to do what he wanted.

Visa obtained, pursuer eluded, a certain tension seemed to lift. 'I never expected to show jazz to a visitor from New Orleans. Especially one so delectable.' This was more like the familiar Leon. 'Your city is one I would much like to visit.'

'Well why not come this year. I'd love to show you round,' Frank said with genuine warmth.

'Alas I cannot. The itinerary is fully determined. But one time I wish to see where King Oliver played when he was with Kid Ory's band.' And he added 'at Pete Lala's' as if Frank cared about the history of every obscure honky-tonk and should immediately cry out in recognition.

She didn't reply. Thoughts were elsewhere. Odd that Delaney's room was so tidy, and yet his habits and appearance were—well, vague for want of a better word. The roar of an approaching train. Where was Leon? A hasty look around. He had moved back, a full five feet from the edge of the platform, as Frank spontaneously edged forward in anticipation of the train.

It was not easy to communicate over the roar. But, as far as she could make out, someone had once tried to push Dr Ivanovitch under a train in the Moscow Subway, and he'd been scared ever since. Whether it had been the KGB or perhaps a short-shifted wife was not made clear.

Leon was now a little jittery. A state that was considerably heightened when a familiar figure dashed on to the platform and just made it into the next carriage, clearly visible through glass dividing door. Pulled out *The Times* and a pen. Frank resisted a temptation to wave.

'How did he find us again?' Leon demanded. 'We lose him at Liverpool Street and here he is again at Green Park two hours later! It is not possible!'

'But he is here,' Frank insisted, with firmness, 'so it is possible.'

'But how is it possible?' Leon rephrased his question.

The only thought in Frank's head just then was an entirely frivolous one. Whether their trilby-ed friend had had any better luck with twelve across.

Leicester Square, get out as planned. 'Dobell's is the best shop. But now they have moved and I cannot remember where it is. So we will try Collett's,' Leon announced, as he led the way up Charing Cross Road, past a stall selling ancient comic books, and up Shaftesbury Avenue. Trilby came along as well, a steady twenty yards behind.

Leon stared in the window of Collett's Jazz Shop in Shaftesbury Avenue. Took a sharp glance back. Their raincoated companion was earnestly studying the menu of a slightly scruffy middle-eastern restaurant.

A sudden sharp intake of breath. Not entirely clear whether it is excitement about *The complete Freddy Keppard*, blue-green album cover on display. No—Dr Ivanovitch has an idea. They enter the store. Leon busies himself with the Classic Jazz rack while Frank, following instructions, goes through door into another shop, Collett's Folk Shop, which fronts on Monmouth Street. Leon quietly follows, silently slides bolt to prevent quick pursuit by that route. There is a taxi waiting outside in Monmouth Street, as if to order. Two travellers collapse into it, laughing. 'But it is not funny,' Leon insists, with wet eyes. 'I come here to buy records and have no chance. Eluding pursuer—mission is successful. Looking for new jazz releases—complete failure!'

Resourceful people these Fellows of Michaelhouse, Frank reflected. Dr Simon Jeffrey, most accomplished burglar, expert safe-cracker. Dr Leon Ivanovitch, master at eluding what seemed like quite a professional 'tail'. What else? Perhaps Dr Bernice Dodds would turn out to be an international-class forger and Professor Andrew Delaney an exceedingly high-class con man. What about Sir Barry Stone, mustn't leave him out. Frank couldn't think of any criminal specialism suitable for the Director.

And one of those Fellows was, in all probability, a fairly top-grade spy. Not to mention a murderer, with a fair amount of imagination and variety in his—or her—repertoire.

'An Indian lunch, I think.' Again Leon didn't consider asking Frank what her preference might be. A package tour must be rather like this, she thought, take the whole thing or leave it.

The taxi crawled up Tottenham Court Road, turned left just before Warren Street Station, stopped outside 'The Volga', of all places. It was an Indian restaurant nevertheless. Leon embarked on a complicated explanation of why *that* name and was joined by the proprietor, Indian consonants and Slavic stress making them sound like a contrapuntal duet. Frank paid no attention at all to the actual words.

They stopped simultaneously. Frank and Leon sat down. Menus. 'The fish we must have.'

Frank, determined to have at least some say, inserted: 'And chicken Madras.'

'You like it hot?' Leon's question was met with a nod.

There were quite a lot of questions Frank would have liked to put to the famous émigré physicist, if she could have had him in an interview situation. Simple straight answers, bash his head on the wall if they weren't forthcoming. Leon Ivanovitch had been somewhat elusive in their contacts over the past week.

'It must have taken a lot of courage to write that letter to *The Washington Post*, Leon?'

'No, it was nothing.' He seemed distinctly uncomfortable. 'Why were we followed today?'

'What did you write about? Sorry, I ought to remember. I do recall one letter demanding better medical attention for a dissident in prison. And one protesting about the invasion of Afghanistan.'

'It is of no consequence.' Question dismissed. Now, Dr Ivanovitch's intonation insisted, listen to what I am talking about. 'Why am I followed? We give him the slip at Liverpool Street and there he is again at Green Park. How? I will tell you.'

Leon leaned across to his blonde companion, who was now in any case giving him full attention. 'He must have known I was going to the Embassy, and was waiting outside when we submerged. No, the word is different. Emerged, that is better.'

Two dishes were placed between them, so hot that the very smell made Frank's eyes start to water. Large bowl of rice, parathas, papadums.

'But if he knows I am going to the Embassy what is the point of following me?'

'Because he didn't know where you might go on to from there, presumably,' Frank suggested. Then, taking advantage of the fact that Leon had a mouthful of curry that was plainly too hot to swallow, why not try a new tack. 'I'd love to hear what it's like working at the Kavendish, Leon. Must be very different from your Institute in Moscow?'

A long draught of water, coursing around the gobbet of meat that still inhabited Leon's mouth. Then he could speak. 'Work is the same everywhere. But that man in the hat. He must have thought I had a secret rendezvous. Who would spy on me? Did he look Russian, do you think?'

Frank was about to suggest that surely a Russian wouldn't do *The Times* crossword when she remembered she was with one who did. But would another . . .

'I think he was English.' Frank tried to be definite just to move the conversation on. 'Perhaps someone is interested in what's happening at the Kavendish. That is the place where great discoveries are made, after all. There must be something interesting going on. Something which people would like to know about. Perhaps they would go so far as stealing . . .'

'The days of Rutherford are past.' Leon tore off a piece of paratha, wrapped it round a couple of strands of chicken and conveyed the package to his mouth. 'Science research is really very dull. You would be bored to detraction if I explained what we are doing.'

'Distraction?' suggested Frank. Leon nodded, as if to say he was glad she agreed with him, now no more on that topic.

Earl Ivanovitch, self-proclaimed. Crooked nose, proud banner of his Jewish lineage. Mustn't be easy being a Jew in Moscow, but Frank supposed he wouldn't want to talk of that either. 'Do you play any games, Leon? To keep fit, I mean.'

'A little squash.' He didn't seem particularly pleased with that question either. 'With Sir Barry Stone. He beats me, although I am five years younger.'

Poor old Leon. But now that he'd started on the fish, which *he* had ordered, good temper seemed to be easing back. 'What do you bet, Frank, that our friend in the raincoat and hat will be waiting outside?'

'I'd be very surprised indeed,' said Frank quite truthfully.

'Have you heard the story of the man who went into a restaurant and ordered soup.' This was better. Reassuring. Let Leon tell a joke. Then perhaps another question or two, although Frank wasn't really terribly hopeful.

'The waiter brought it and he had his thumb in the soup. "What do you mean?" the customer cried, "putting your thumb in my soup!" The waiter explained: "I have a boil on my thumb, and it eases the pain to immerse it in a hot liquid."'

Frank gave the joke thirty per cent of her attention. It was important to think about the report she'd have to give in a couple of hours. To Lord Johns and perhaps also the Prime Minister. Things were, at last, falling into place. Just one more day—surely not an unreasonable request?

'"So you put your diseased thumb in my soup!" the diner shouted in anger. "Why do you not stick it up your bum?" "I do," said the waiter, "when I'm not carrying soup."'

Frank wasn't sure what their waiter—who was just then handing Leon his bill with a slight bow—thought of all this.

But Leon was now in high spirits. 'We will not eat ice-cream here. It is the English variety, made with lard. There is an American ice-cream parlour—' he pronounced the words with relish, even with Kentucky-flavoured vowels, '—just down Tottenham Court Road.'

Dr Ivanovitch had originally planned to inveigle Ms le Roux into the YMCA at Russell Square for perhaps an hour. Fun and games. She could say no, but nothing lost in trying. He looked wistfully at the building, little individual bedrooms. 'In America one can rent a room by the hour. A realistic country.'

'Nothing like that here,' Frank reminded him firmly. 'Come on, I'm having a Butter Pecan.'

'It would be too dangerous today, with all the following,' Leon rationalised in an undertone intended mainly for himself. And then he entered into the great American ice-cream tasting ritual. A tiny blob of Blueberry Pie on a plastic spatula. Then Rocky Road, and a morsel of Pacific Pearl before settling for a Pistachio. Leon Ivanovitch always opted for Pistachio, but it was good to sample some of the others.

Leon was now going to talk to colleagues at the University of London. Might there be some mention of Pasars? Unlikely. He wouldn't have brought Frank along if that had been his plan. Why on earth *had* he invited her? For company—of a spiritual or physical nature? The day hadn't been at all wasted as far as Frank was concerned, but for Leon . . .

Harmless chatter about jazz as they walked up Gower Street, half of it lost in the roar of traffic. University College, with its imposing Greek front. No—a façade. Truly, as Leon gently dissuaded Frank from ascending the magnificent steps. 'Those doors are not used. Here, we come around the side. They will still be drinking coffee.'

They were. Just like Cambridge, meal times must go on for about two hours. Nigel Schmidt and Karen Oates greeted Leon warmly, Frank even more so. And there was a third mathematician present, who didn't seem at all surprised at meeting her there. Andrew Delaney, pops up everywhere I go.

'No more narrow escapes, Frank?' Delaney enquired.

'What do you mean?'

'You haven't forgotten old John Fisher almost squashing us flat. And you could have been in that pink punt with Simon if I hadn't rescued you.' Well, if she'd worked it out, why shouldn't he. But if *he* had dropped the bomb would Andrew now talk about it? 'Not to mention that poisoned potation that you just missed drinking. I should think that at the very least you'd have been almost hit by some falling scaffolding in London today. Or just escaped being pushed under a tube train.'

Leon Ivanovitch, at these words, turned extremely white. Took a quick drink of coffee which went straight down the wrong pipe and left him coughing and spluttering with plain Dr Karen Oates vigorously thumping his back—bang, bang, like a gym mistress.

Frank excused herself. The telephone was nearby, guarded by Jeremy Bentham—life-size wax image including his actual skeleton, sitting in a glass case, his skull in a box by his feet.

Lord Johns' ever-ready number had a message, venue for the

three o'clock appointment. Just nice time, twenty minutes in a taxi.

The Prime Minister, his Lordship said, sent her apologies. Something about a crisis over pay for coal miners. And British Leyland. Things like that. Waved away as details fit only for Prime Ministers. 'Now,' he lit a cigar, puffed it straight at Frank. 'What about Pasars?'

Well, she reflected, it probably is more important than an automobile company which spends so much time on strike that the models are out-of-date before they actually get manufactured.

Some fairly definite report was required. Frank had a hypothesis—as Barry Stone would say, amazing how jargon rubs off on one in the short space of a week. She outlined to Lord Johns the only possible solution that tied together *almost* everything that had happened. Stressed the 'almost'.

Three or four questions remained, information that might help to clinch things. Lord Johns had the answer to one, the right answer too. He got almost excited—as much as anyone from Eton and Michaelhouse could get honest-to-goodness, pent-up, losing-his-cool excited. But a well-supported idea—Frank had to remind his Lordship—isn't proof. Twenty-four hours more. Give the spy a bit of rope—invitation to hang him- (or of course her-) self. Extend the invitation to all suspects. Stone, Ivanovitch, Delaney, Dodds and petite Louise Bates. Only most especially to one particular, putatively unpatriotic person. Twenty-four hours more and we should have the whole thing sewn up. (Unless I get sewn up, in a shroud, at the end of that time. Frank expunged the thought.)

Lord Johns would be there as well. All the better, since you're really a suspect too, Frank told him with her eyes. 'The May Ball. Never miss the May Ball. In fact I was going to ask if you'd be my partner. My wife was coming but she's got caught up in a Paediatricians' Congress. Can you imagine anything more boring?'

His Lordship wouldn't actually be leaving until five. Had to finish a day's work at the office first, don't you know. Frank really didn't, especially after the two large ports he'd put away while talking to her. But it did leave a little time for Frank to savour Señor Dali.

She almost wished she hadn't. Gelatinous watches, bones into boiled beans, a grand piano merged with a skull. These were all right. But 'The Angel of Death', skeleton on horseback by a black cliff, framed by rainbow. Frank shivered as she climbed into the back of the lordly Mercedes, chauffeur up front, and acceded to a suggestion that she 'call me Harry, going to a ball together and all that, don't you know'.

A lot of idle talk about Cambridge and Tripos examinations. Touristy fill-in about University policemen called Proctors, and Bulldogs (who were really men) and why most May Balls were held in June, only Michaelhouse being truly literal.

There was one question that surely the burly chauffeur could be permitted to overhear. And Frank demanded a straight, plain answer.

'Harry.' To soften him in advance. 'Harry, why is the Mastership of Michaelhouse so highly valued? Every single person I've talked to would give anything for it. Including you,' she reminded him.

'Well,' he considered, 'it's a very important, traditional office.'

'I want an answer.'

'You won't be impressed, Frank.'

'I still want it.'

His Lordship turned to look out of the window. Flat fields and power lines and new towns. 'It's the cellar. They started laying down good wine in the fifteenth century. Definitely the oldest and without doubt the finest collection of vintage wines in the whole of England.'

'You don't have any five-hundred-year-old wines, surely?' Frank wrinkled her nose at the thought.

'Oh no,' Lord Harry hastened to clarify. 'But there are thought to be some seventeenth-century brandies. And the finest old Aloxe Corton in the world. You see,' he lowered his voice and now looked directly at Frank, 'only the Master has the keys. Every bottle of wine is fetched by him individually. No one else may enter. That is the strictest tradition of all.'

Frank could think of absolutely nothing to say.

'There,' Lord Johns added, lamely. The first time she'd really seen him discomforted. Or any of the other Fellows, for that matter, with the occasional exception of Leon. 'There, I said you wouldn't be impressed.'

XI

IT WAS LIKE coming back to a different age. One huge white marquee set right in the middle of Michaelhouse Front Court, filling almost the entire quadrangle. Its centre pole thirty, maybe forty feet high, dwarfing the baronial dining hall, making Michaelhouse's revered mediaeval buildings look like a cardboard backdrop, hurriedly erected for some low-budget Hollywood comedy.

Thank goodness I've been invited, as Frank looked out of her window at the network of ropes holding up the vast tent. Like Ringling Brothers and Barnum and Bailey. One almost expected to see a convoy of elephants trumpeting through the Michaelhouse front gate, trunks waving in anticipation, leopard-skin-clad tight-rope artists balancing on one leg on their calloused backs.

From ten o'clock until six in the morning. Music all the way, Lord Harry had told her—with a relish that seemed unbecoming to his office, his age, his very nationality. Not much chance of sleep this near the bandstand, and not much fun dancing in one's own room when everyone else is at the party.

There wasn't much more thinking to be done, not until she'd seen what happened at the ball. Most of the pieces seemed to fit together with only a small amount of forcing. It was just a pity that they didn't seem *all* to belong to the same puzzle.

Frank finished *The Masters*, and slept for two hours. A deep slumber, woken only by a dream figure who seemed a blend of President Reagan and Dr Leon Ivanovitch, ascending slowly into the sky. Pasar power in them thar thousand-dollar cowboy boots? Maybe—the only thing was that he was yelling something, an urgent and desperate cry, in a language Frank didn't understand.

Ball time. All the men in tuxedos—except that the English didn't call them that. Frank put on the same long red dress she'd worn for the Ffothergill-Hawthorn-Williams Feast. Sequined sleeves. She'd bought it for Mardi Gras the year before last, having then just got back in New Orleans from uncovering a racket in illicit whale farming, patent breach of the international agreement. Piece of cake compared with operating in an English university city, where people would commit bloody murder for a cellarful of old wines. Or did they? Which was more important to Stone and Harry Johns and Delaney—ancient brandy or the untold wonders of Pasar Power? It didn't bear thought.

Lord Johns was wearing a pink carnation, and presented another to Frank, pinning it carefully to her dress, pink on red. The first number was slow and it was possible to waltz. No one else was; just slow, sinuous jive. Oh yes they were—Sir Barry Stone and that must surely be his wife, Lady Stone, the well-known plumber. Frank waved and so did Sir Barry, while Lord Johns merely lifted one affable finger in salute.

'Three musical groups will alternate throughout the evening.' Lord Johns sounded like an announcer on high-brow Radio Three. The first was billed as 'Three Hugs and a Cuddle'. A trio of mountainous hairy men playing what looked in their hands like dwarf instruments—electric guitar, bass and drums. Lord Johns really was at a ball, Pasars banished entirely from conversation (although surely not from thoughts). Well, he hadn't been threatened and nearly squashed or bombed or poisoned umpteen times in the last week. Frank danced—almost swam across the plank floor—with nerves tingling.

Whipcrack roll on the drums. Frank jumped. Felt she might hit her head on the ornate crystal (or imitation thereof) chandelier that was suspended above their heads. (Must have a bit of class in the tent, by jove, for the Michaelhouse May Ball.) A fanfare—if one can have a fanfare on an electric guitar—heralded the arrival on stage of a short, slightly plump singer with patently false blond hair, dressed in white woolly trousers and gottcha. The Cuddle, no less. She actually had been christened Mavis Cuddle, the bass-player averred to anyone who cared, or could pick out his Glasgow tones through the jarry amplification.

Lord Harry Johns needed a drink. 'All this champagne, better get started before it begins to warm up.' Frank was claimed for the next dance by a familiar face. Yorkshire accent tonight. The better he dressed, the more low-down the voice?

'Haven't seen you for a long time,' Simon Jeffrey began.

No, not since you waved to me about two seconds before Sampson Ndagbera was blasted into whatever hereafter he believed in. But why not try to forget about Saturday altogether.

'Hey, I really enjoyed our escapade on Friday night, Simon. Pity it didn't turn up what you were looking for.'

Mavis Cuddle was beginning on a distinctly sentimental note:

The wind was whispering,
Birds were singing,
All one song . . .

If only she would whisper too. That voice, akin to a strangulated goat, seemed a trifle incongruous coming from someone who looked like Little Bo-Peep. Now if she'd dyed her hair red . . .

'What were you looking for, Simon?' Frank persisted, steering him to an almost dead corner of the tent, just out of reach of high-blown amplification.

'Well why shouldn't I tell you, Frank.' The song stopped. They sat on a bench. Better. Hard to talk at the same time as wiggling hips and knees, making a fake mating invitation at one's partner, as demanded by the social conventions of the late twentieth century.

'I know there's a secret because I went through Pat Most's rooms. One night when he was off digging it into bare-breasted Bernice. Behind his fireplace he had eight pages in a brown envelope.'

'So you photocopied them,' Frank suggested.

'No, nothing like that.' One could almost hear Uncle Mose protesting at what the hell was the world coming to! You couldn't photocopy jewellery, or gold, or bank notes. (Not quite yet, anyway.) 'I just took 'em.' Simon made it seem so simple. 'Put 'em behind my fireplace.' Where else?

'And you were looking in the Kavendish for . . .'

'For more. It was physics, I could tell that. About something called P. That's all it said. P for perfect secret.'

Simon Jeffrey had been sitting next to Frank in the Union when the first note reached her. He certainly couldn't have dropped a bomb on his own punt. Was Simon really what he seemed—still a schoolboy at heart? Uncle Mose's nephew, playing harmless games in the margins of a real-life death and espionage drama? Why not, everything pointed to that interpretation. Why wouldn't Frank accept it?

The Cuddle returned, this time immersed in yellow like a chicken just hatched, licking off the yolk. Tempo gradually hardening. Take away the posh accents and Michaelhouse students were no different from those yobos who'd tried to snatch the punt-pole from Delaney. No different from kids in Chicago or Sydney or—although Frank hadn't yet been to check up on that particular scene—surely no different from kids in Leningrad.

'Look at old Andrew across there with Johnsie-boy,' Simon remarked. 'Lobbying for the Mastership I'll be bound. Election's tomorrow, you know.'

Mavis the Cuddle was into another set of instantly forgettable words, voice like a rusty axle:

I want to read the news on the tee-vee,
I'll tell the world about you . . .

'Who're you going to vote for, Simon?' And who would Uncle Mose have voted for? Or is that the same question.

'Oh, Andy Delaney without doubt. Wouldn't want Bernice having month-long initiation rites in our cellar, no thank you. Deflowering virgins with bottles of vintage Burgundy, indeed!'

Surely she's got to have something new up her sleeve for the fourth edition, Frank refrained from suggesting.

'Who would you vote for, Frank?' Simon decided that two could ask questions. And for his part he had answered straightaway, right off the cuff.

Frank wasn't exactly nonplussed, she just hadn't thought about it. Surely any arbitrary answer would do. She wouldn't be giving anything away? Nothing in her subconscious that she was scarcely aware of? No, of course not.

'Bernice.'

'Why?'

Hell. Because you wouldn't. Because she's a woman—no, it did sound a bit funny as the total reason. Try another tack. Might elicit a useful response, you never know.

'I'd be worried about Andrew. After all he is a communist.'

Cuddles was now intoning how she'd also refer to her love for 'that man' within the format of the weather forecast, BBC permitting. Frowns on the brow followed by clear intervals on left cheek and a sunny smile, intermittently, after dark? No such subtlety from our Mavis, most unfortunately.

'Communist, schmomunist.' Simon now imitated a Yorkshireman imitating a Jewish accent from Brooklyn. 'That's just a game. Because mathematical research doesn't take more than three hours out of the day.'

Further clarification of the connection—if indeed any were possible—between these two statements was circumvented by the arrival of Comrade Delaney in person, to claim Frank for a decadent capitalist-style dance. More like neodecadent, now that the relatively mild sound of Mavis Cuddle and her hulking companions was to be replaced by a group announced as 'Burns, Scalds and Boils'. To tumultous approbation from the—must now be two hundred—students, in pose already to recommence gyration.

'Good dance Andrew, hey?'

'It's sad, Frankie, a bit too sad.'

Burns, Scalds and Boils turned out to be four diminutive youths—pale-faced, clean-shaven, clumps of acne plainly visible. In skin-tight pure-white one-piece costumes.

'Poor old Sampson,' Delaney expanded. 'Bombed to death on Saturday, buried yesterday and here we are dancing through the night. It's not really—well, it's not decent, is it?'

'But the ball was organised a long time ago. Bands booked.

And the students . . .' Frank tried to be matter-of-fact. There was also the murder of Patrick Most. Was that quite forgotten? Or didn't it matter?

'Yes, but *we* didn't have to *come*.' Professor Delaney hissed the words at her, over the increasingly frenetic sound being put out by those four mild-looking youths.

Frank surveyed the scene. Simon was now dancing with his partner of the night, Louise. James Thorpe just that moment walked in. Looked quite bewildered. Was this what students did? Including students who would live in the new wing to be built by his money. Hard-earned pounds from the car-rental market, to provide sleeping places for people who could really enjoy dancing to this . . . noise? That was what Mr Thorpe's face seemed to say. Then the aged benefactor's features mellowed, even smiled, as he was led into a quiet corner by Bernice. Plied with champagne. She might even get him to dance. Later on, of course. Dance the money off him.

Sir Barry and Lady S. were now dancing like the students, and doing it well, too. Nothing like jumping down a generation.

What was that? Familiar face. Yes, yes—Roger, of the resounding laugh. Together with Deirdre, although he didn't seem to be paying too much attention to her. Peeping around the room. For what? And how, Frank asked herself, did someone who sold fruit in the market find fifty pounds for a May Ball ticket?

'What were you doing in London with Ivanovitch, anyway?' Delaney's attention was directed entirely towards his partner.

'Oh well,' it couldn't help sounding rather lame, 'he just invited me. Leon wanted moral support at the Embassy.'

The pimpliest Burn—or could he be a Scald—was now mouthing words over the relentless beat. At least they had a certain appropriateness.

You make my blood boil,
And my heart go . . . zoom,
My liver-er's jumping,
When you squeeze me so-ó-ó-ó . . .

Andrew Delaney. Effete patrician; communist, whatever it means to be a Communist in Britain. Exceptional mathematician. Someone who could have a fair entry to Pasar secrets if he so chose. But he didn't, or said he didn't.

Delaney had been with Frank when John Fisher's head fell from on high. So he couldn't have pushed it off. If, indeed, anyone had. He'd been ensconced on the Union platform when the first threatening note had arrived. What about Sampson's murder? Certainly, there had been time for Delaney to reach his room, gather up a bomb, walk over to Staircase K and aim it at the pink punt. Delaney was the only person who knew it wasn't Frank in that vessel of pleasure. If he *had* done it only Sampson could have been the intended victim.

'He's got two wives, you know, back in Russia. And he makes a pass at every female student here. Highly embarrassing for the college.'

It took Frank a moment to focus on the object of Delaney's slightly jealous grumble.

'I think Leon is quite sweet,' she said, truthfully. So let's have no more of that sniping. 'And he did tell me all about those two wives. I'm sure it's no odder than lots of things which go on around Cambridge.'

Time for supper. No event at Cambridge would be complete without generous quantities of food. Trestle tables were quickly erected on the dance floor. Lace tablecloths. Nests of chairs carried in by black-bow-tied student organisers.

'Frank, would you care to join us?' Sir Barry Stone, Senior Fellow until the election tomorrow afternoon. No, today—Frank's watch stood at quarter after midnight. Would he then be Master? Or would Delaney? Or delectable Bernice Dodds, now being escorted to the same table by Andrew Delaney, her official partner for the Ball.

'I'd like you to meet my wife. Frank le Roux. Dr Pamela Stone.' A very smart-looking lady, hair grey in a distinguished way, bright brown eyes. Firm handshake.

Doctor? Delaney said she was a plumber. He'd said so twice, quite distinctly.

The puzzlement must have shown in Frank's face. Damn it, I really ought to be more careful.

'I'm not a medical doctor. It's just a PhD in Engineering.' Well modulated voice, still recognisably Queensland. Interesting the way he'd introduced her as Dr Pamela, rather than Lady S. Treating her as a person in her own right. Well, these Australians certainly weren't all hoggishly chauvinistic, Frank noted.

'Pammy runs the government standards laboratory at Saffron Walden. Testing strengths of pipes and joints and things.'

Damn Delaney, Frank decided, and all ultra-snobbish English intellectuals. Just because Pamela Stone worked with something other than abstractions. Maybe just because, despite being a woman, she did *work*. Calling her a plumber was like saying Ike was a GI. Highly insulting, for one thing.

Real bone china plates. None of your throw-away plastic whatsits for the Michaelhouse May Ball Midnight Supper. Why not Midnight Feast? No, that word had a far grander connotation in Cambridge. Anyway, people got murdered at Feasts. But not—Frank crossed her fingers, almost crossed herself—at midnight suppers. Please not!

A Chinese banquet from the Michaelhouse chef. Easy sort of food to prepare in quantity, Louise ventured, as she sat down on Frank's other side. Bernice was across the table, looking—Frank had to admit—rather ravishing in an emerald green dress, neckline plunging to just an inch or two above her navel. She was still acting in loco parentis for James Thorpe. Food, his eyes gave a glimmer of recognition. Mr Thorpe knew what that was—something which was necessary to get you from one accounting period to the next.

Conversation during the first part of the meal was vapid. Unenlightening to Frank across whose brain beat one word in persistent tattoo: 'Pasar, Pasar, Pasar . . .' Champagne only made it louder, deeper, like the drip-drip of Chinese torture. China—ah, indeed!

Sweet and sour prawn. Would they have noticed if it was sweet and sour Fellow? Frank had a vivid image of the members of Michaelhouse High Table steadily succumbing to their doom, until there was but one left. Solemnly sitting all by him- (or perhaps her-) self, commenting on the quality of the wine, denigrating modern trends. . . .

'. . . of free contraception for all.' Beatrice had found a topic about which to wax fiery. 'Did you know that in Cambridge a fifteen-year-old can get a prescription for the pill and the doctor is obliged *not* to tell her parents.'

'That's not quite right,' Dr Pamela Stone suggested. 'Our doctor . . .'

'Why shouldn't they? It's their bodies.' Thus spake the voice of youth. Petite youth at that, albeit hard-boiled, all-knowing. And caring? Louise Bates looked across at Frank for support. Unforthcoming. Some people—Frank didn't even feel like saying it—some people like to keep their sexual proclivities and opinions modestly tucked away.

'I still say that sex should be an adult pleasure, not a game for children,' Bernice said.

'Oh come on,' Louise responded. 'What about all those societies in Africa and Australia you talk about in your book. The girls there do it at thirteen, or twelve.'

'Louise, those girls have to behave like adults at that age. They have responsibilities. Gathering food and firewood. Cooking. Then they have children at fourteen or fifteen. People do grow up quicker in primitive societies. And for them sex is a highly responsible act. It seals a marriage. That's why they have such elaborate rituals. Our society is totally lacking in ritual.'

Oh I don't know, Frank decided against saying. Getting up the nerve to creep into a motel. Quarters in the video to call up a porno movie. Bit of ritual there, surely? Speaking as a sociologist to an anthropologist, of course.

Louise did respond: 'We have a different attitude to things, that's all. We are not primitive, that's the important thing. What's wrong with a bit of sexual fun before you have to settle down to the dull grind of bringing up a family?'

'America's the worst example,' Bernice continued unperturbed. 'The sexual act is so lightly valued that they've almost lost the ability to do it. Hence the continual search for new partners. Novelty helps, for a time or two. And porno movies in motel rooms. Tsst!'

Pretty lucky I didn't say it, Frank blessed her caution.

'That is highly arguable.' Louise tried hard to remember to observe the rules of debate. Rather than, say, scratching Bernice's eyes out. 'America is the most advanced country in the world today. The highest standard of living. We set the pace. People look up to us, trust us.'

'This lady doesn't.' Bernice kept her voice low and cool. 'I wouldn't trust you with the secret of where I'd hidden my Easter eggs.'

Now who had said anything about secrets? Unfortunately, just at that moment Lady Stone decided that as Senior Fellow's wife she should intervene. Stop bloodshed, that sort of thing.

'Barry and I love America,' she tried to gush like an American, but with only mild success. 'I can't get away from my job for more than three months at a time so he has most of his sabbaticals here in Cambridge. We did spend a term at Princeton, though, last year.'

She obtained what was perhaps the required effect. Complete silence from the two combatants. Louise pointedly asked Simon to pass the crispy noodles while Bernice began once more fawning over James Thorpe, who was valiantly trying to convey food to mouth with one chopstick held in each hand.

'China is where I've always wanted to visit,' continued Lady P., talking now exclusively to Frank.

'Why, to see the plumbing?' Frank realised she hadn't really meant to say that.

'Yes,' Dr Stone agreed. It had been the right question! 'Especially their venting systems . . .'

And so it went on. Frank always did find it interesting to chat with the wives of men she'd bedded—it was the sociologist in her, no doubt. But only for about ten minutes. Longer than that could become painful. Pamela Stone finished the mini-lecture on partial vacuums and pressure differential. Questions about Frank's mother. Her late father—how did he die? What a dreadful fate, to be bitten by an alligator. Her sometime husband. Hobbies. Books recently read . . .

Sitting there under the huge chandelier, now rotating, beams of light crossing and interweaving over the centre table. The Stones. Bernice and Delaney. Louise and Simon. Old James Thorpe, humourless but contented. Lord Harry Johns and Frank le Roux. Leon Ivanovitch and his partner of the evening, a languorous, black-haired PhD student called Tanya. Almost exactly the gathering from that Feast of the Apparition of St Michael, last Wednesday. Just two missing. Just two dead.

Ping-ping-ping. Lord Johns banged fork against champagne glass as the last plates were cleared away. Immaculate waiter from High Table dressed tonight in a maroon jacket just to emphasise that the occasion was slightly frivolous, not entirely formal. Certainly not an official bequest Feast.

'A toast. To our guest from across the Atlantic, Frank le Roux. Here's luck to her, in finding out what exactly goes on behind those high fences at the Kavendish.' Simon looked across at Frank, gave her a broad Yorkshire wink.

Glasses were raised, clinked, sipped, as a small delicacy was placed before each guest on the centre table. This was on a paper plate. 'A traditional American custom,' Lord Harry explained, 'a Chinese Fortune Cookie.' The slight emphasis on 'Chinese' would perhaps only have been caught by someone whose mind was definitely thinking along those lines. Frank le Roux. And, surely, one other person at that table.

It was impossible to watch everyone at once. Harry Johns and Frank had agreed each to pay closest attention to those at their own end of the table.

Leon Ivanovitch was still slightly reeling from the shock of unlimited food, endless variety, novel tastes. Leon bit first, extracted a thin folded piece of paper. Larger than the customary sliver. A note, neat black lettering: GO HOME YANK above a skull and crossbones in red.

Coloured photocopy of the note that had been passed down to Frank le Roux in the Cambridge Union last Thursday. She'd have preferred the one from the blackboard but that had been erased. And you couldn't put a blackboard in a cookie. This did look like—was supposed to appear to be—the real thing.

'What is it? I am no Yank.' There seemed a note of sorrow in his voice. 'It is some crazy Cambridge joke, no?' Leon looked around for guidance.

Everyone else was busy unfolding their fortunes. Identical insertion in each. Someone—Frank had argued and Lord Johns wholeheartedly agreed—would think it was the note he (or she) had penned. Someone would react accordingly.

Andrew Delaney turned deathly pale, fortified himself with a draught of champagne, directed a stare across at Lord Johns, and remarked: 'I don't think this is at all funny.'

Louise looked straight at Bernice. Looked daggers, as if it were entirely her doing.

Leon, true scientist that he was, demanded an explicit explanation. 'From World War Two it must be? A romantic note, for international solidarity, no?'

Simon stammered for the first time in Frank's hearing. Ordinary Cambridge accent, Yorkshire veneer forgotten in his surprise. 'What d-d-does it m-mean?' The question was addressed to Frank.

Sir Barry Stone smoothed out his message. Read it impassively. Looked over at Dr Pamela's. Deliberately placed both notes together. Folded over once, tore into eight pieces, the bits dismissively sprinkled over the dance floor.

Bernice was last to read the threatening note. Mouthed the words as she did. Finished with a blank look in her eyes, mouth open as if to speak. Then Dr Dodds' attention was quickly diverted to old James Thorpe who had eaten the whole cookie, note and all, and was now mildly choking. 'Spit it out!' she had to shout, twice, into his good left ear.

Time for more music. Dancing and jollity must recommence. Frank wished that she felt in those spirits. Tired, that was the correct word to describe her physical state. Being mentally dispirited didn't help. Find a murderer and jump over the moon? And how!

Sir Barry, having obtained Lady Pamela's permission, offered

Frank his arm. Began with waltz-step because it was easier to talk that way. Three grizzly-bear-like minstrels strummed and drummed their way into tune and then a red bundle, a pompom with head and legs, bounded into the spotlight. Mavis the Cuddle. Her name was probably really Kadel, Hungarian or suchlike, Frank reflected, trying to think analytically about something.

'How goes it Frankie? You don't seem to be enjoying our frolic as much as a young thing like you should.'

'No? Sorry, Barry, it really is a great experience.' Frank managed a smile. Thinnish, but better than nothing.

'Any luck?'

Frank had little heart for asking questions, still less for answering.

'Come on then!' The music quickened and so did Sir Barry. Swinging knees and hands and hips from side to side. Frank responded, or she was aware that her body did.

Make a try. There was still so much that she didn't know. How in six days could one learn enough to understand the significance of Pasars, their international value? It was like trying to do a jigsaw puzzle without any picture on the pieces, just shapes, the same ones recurring, could go here or here or here.

'Whenabouts would you expect Pasars to be in production, Barry?'

'Early next year.' He had to say it twice over the unCuddlesome whine. Did someone turn the amplifiers up? Or was Frank just getting deafer as the night wore relentlessy on.

'Wow! And they'll be used for?'

'Lighting and heating in the Outer Hebrides. As a pilot project. There's an old aircraft factory near Bristol that could be converted for a million or so. Cabinet should be making a decision next month.'

I'd like to pick you up and turn you upside down,
Shake, shake, shake till all the spun' comes down,
I'm going to make you the man for me,
To satisfy me all I pleeeezzzz.

Little Mavis darted from one large Hug to the next delivering this ultimatum. She'd need a crane to achieve that ambition, Frank decided.

'And there'll be a pilot train, an automobile engine, and a light aircraft propulsion unit. By about the middle of next year. The basic principles are all there in the Pasar papers. Detailed design shouldn't take more than six months. The whole joy of Pasars is everything is so simple.'

And how long would a bomb take to make, Frank wondered to herself. Less time, probably. Trains have to stay on rails, cars stop and start, a plane must come down safely. But all a bomb has to do is go off. And the less control the better.

Sir Barry now returned to the side-bench where Lady Pamela had taken over as custodian of Mr Thorpe. For someone who had seldom touched liquor in his hard-working life, or so he said, mister money-bags had a remarkable ability to remain sober. Pamela Stone, super-plumber, steadily sipped a tall tumbler of iced water as she replenished Mr Thorpe's mug—how had he got a mug?—with champagne.

Lord Johns demanded a dance. He was after all paying for Frank's night of fun. Had paid for her to come to England, out of the Federal pocket over which he watched. And it wasn't so much a dance he wanted as a progress report.

'No positive reactions my end, Frank.'

'No.' One might just as well accept defeat gracefully, as have it forced upon one, Frank reflected. 'I'm quite certain that no one had seen that note before.' Pity we couldn't have used the blackboard threat. But perhaps no one would have recognised that either. Perhaps no one here killed Most or Sampson. Maybe it was all divine intervention. Frank's mind swam. Faster than Mavis Cuddle could wiggle, up there on the platform, looking now like a large round red football that was being bounced on the spot.

'Harry, I'm sorry I'm proving so inept at this.'

'Not at all, not at all.' Reassuring words at night, sure. But that wouldn't avoid the ignomy of being sacked in the sober light of tomorrow. Packed off home in defeat, reputation tarnished.

British Government's secret broadcast to the furthest corner of the world.

'What you explained to me in London *does* hang together. I've ordered investigation of those points you listed. There should be a report through quite soon.'

Then Lord Johns made an appointment to meet Frank at nine fifteen in the morning. Funny sort of place for a rendezvous, she thought. He stopped pretending to dance and went off in course of duty to join the Stones at their Thorpe-charming.

Three Hugs and One Cuddle disappeared from the bandstand. Short intermission while a new set of drums was assembled. Jazz band on stage. Real genuine jazz band, if a group of white men, white Englishmen, can be called genuine. At jazz that is.

'Now it must be my turn, my pleasure.'

Leon Ivanovitch, divested of jacket and tie and collar. Why not time for a bit of fun, Frank thought, as Leon took her hand, spun her round, guided back under arched arm. Dance, just dance . . .

'We should forget all about work, Leon.' He grinned in reply. 'Forget all about secrets.' No response to this. Had he heard? Why do I try, Frank asked herself, as Leon began singing words to the song. His own words.

'Eyes are green, shoes are green, we all scream for ice cream.'

'No, no,' Frank laughed, as the trumpet player did begin to sing. To sing the same words as Frank. 'Ice cream, you scream, we all scream for ice cream.'

'Perhaps,' said Leon with unbecoming lack of dogmatism. 'But I think I prefer my words.'

Dance, Frank told herself. Dance, enjoy, stretch. Suppress mind, ideas, worries, fears. Andrew Delaney was cavorting like a beanstalk with sad-eyed Deirdre. Barry Stone with Louise—smooth, fluent, blending together. Bernice now partnered by Simon, danced around him as if it were a sacrificial ritual. Dr Jeffrey to be mesmerised, raped by ten virgins then cut into ten pieces and chewed, delicately, the gristle being made into gut for magical bows that would transduce any enemy.

Dr Leon Ivanovitch. Could have killed Patrick Most. Could

have tried to kill Delaney and Frank with a large, square, heavy block of sixteenth-century carving. Could easily have bombed his star student, Sampson Ndagbera, the white hope of the third world. (Could a black man be a white hope? Frank filed away the question.)

It would have been hard for Leon to have initiated the note in the Union, since he was speaking out front at the time. And anyway, to 'Go Home Yank' he'd as like as not have added 'and please take me with you'. Americophile, that was Dr Ivanovitch. Ice cream, New Orleans jazz and motels that rent by the hour.

Slower tune. Clarinetist sings, white man trying to sound like black, like American black:

If you want to taste, pleasures that are sweet,

Leon danced closer to Frank. Eyes spoke. Bedroom eyes.

Come to New Orleans, visit Bourbon Street.

Delaney still with Deirdre. Dead centre. Smooching, bodies pressed together, scarcely moving from one spot.

Hell, why not, Frank was weighing up. There's nothing to lose and there might well be considerable . . .

One huge chandelier descended. Fell two feet. Stopped. Then started to fall again. Fast, gathering speed. Frank watched, transfixed, mouth open to yell a warning but throat frozen. Delaney and Deirdre under the light. Huge glass and metal contraption careering towards plank floor. Delaney tries at the last minute to escape, throws back his torso but feet appear rooted to the spot. Deirdre jumps neatly, emits a single high-pitched scream as Andrew Delaney collapses to the floor, one leg transfixed by the glorious mark of quality from the Michael-house May Ball.

His eyes were closed but as Lord Johns soon verified—assuming what by now seemed to be his customary medical role at Michaelhouse social events—there was a pulse. Normal pulse. Broken leg. Shock. Mild concussion as head had hit ground. Nothing really to worry about, Leon reported when he returned to Frank after a quick word with Lord Harry. The Professor of

Pure Mathematics was carried out on one stretcher and the chandelier on another.

A three-ply rope had fallen across the floor. The rope which had held the chandelier in position. Through a hole in the apex of the marquee and down the far side, fastened at ground level. One rope with its end cut. Neatly cut. Cut with a good sharp knife.

XII

NEXT MORNING, WEDNESDAY morning, awoke with a grey sky. Very light drizzle. What the British call rain but would be passed over in New Orleans as just like a communal shower. Refreshing, cooling. In Cambridge it felt simply damp and miserable. Frank's mood, to a T.

Three hours of sleep had left her feeling plain woozy. Three cups of hot black coffee made no difference whatsoever. Frank got up mechanically. Dressed. Picked up bag. Patted it for reassurance, almost empty reassurance. Walked out into the dank morning, around the edge of the court, stepping over tent pegs of the huge, empty, sorrowful marquee. No way now to avoid a falling gargoyle.

Students attired as if for a formal dinner were earnestly headed for tripos exams. Walking down the centre of Trinity Street, gowns flapping, mortar boards to keep the rain off, each studying a crib. Repeating formulas in quantum mechanics, irregular verbs in Greek; dates, times, symbolic incantations; knowledge, facts and myth.

Across the street to Heffer's main bookstore. Past piles of *Primitive Procreation*, signed by the author, no extra charge. I should write a book, Frank decided. How to let everyone around you get murdered. Secrets stolen. And do nothing. Should be a best-seller. I could autograph each copy in blood. At least I couldn't be any less successful as a writer than I am as a detective.

Still—she essayed a bit of self-cheer past a table of poetry anthologies—it really wasn't for lack of trying. And I had so *nearly* got it solved. The jigsaw almost complete and then someone had to go and kick the table.

Nine fifteen, he'd said, over in the far corner by the Oceanic section. Frank descended into Heffer's basement. Past Linguistics, Latin, Greek, Chinese. She was early but Lord Johns was already there, deep in a history of the Wesleyan Church in Tonga.

Frank pretended to browse, although there seemed no one else in that obscure corner of the store, at that time in the morning. *A grammar of Yidin.* What is heaven's name is that? Spoken by the Aborigines of Australia. Oh, so that is where the thirteenth tribe of Israel strayed to . . . .

'The police have charged a youth called Roger Dodson with attempted manslaughter of Professor Delaney. By cutting the rope that held the chandelier in position. He's in custody now.'

It really was like a spy story. Lord Johns spoke at right-angles to Frank, into his book. Told the news to a picture of King George Tubou I of Tonga.

'How's Andrew, Harry?' Frank addressed the remark to a photo of two fat laughing Aboriginal ladies. Well, part Aboriginal. But certainly darker than Frank.

'He's fine. Simple fracture of the tibia. About a week in hospital. Another couple of weeks in plaster and he'll be right as rain.'

Frank flipped over the pages. She wasn't used to talking to people, being talked to, without being able to look them in the eye.

'Dodson was annoyed about Delaney dancing with a girl. Someone who he'd brought to the ball himself.'

'Yes, Deirdre,' Frank supplied.

'Apparently Dodson was known to Delaney. Used to be a student of his.'

Of course. Most murders and attempted murders, and rapes and things like that, are committed by friends or relatives. You've got to have some reason for hating. 'So Roger was jealous of the attention Delaney was paying to Deirdre?'

Harry Johns' voice was clipped, precise, businesslike. And those upper-echelon vowels gave it the ring of total authority. 'He was jealous, I'm told. But Dodson apparently had no feelings at all for the girl Deirdre.'

Frank waited, flipped over a page to some mind-baffling linguistic formula.

'He had a crush, you could say, on Delaney. The police went through Andrew's pockets and found a—' Lord Johns paused, in delicate distaste, '—a love letter from Dodson.'

'Signed Dodger,' Frank suggested, her soft Louisianan timbre making the information appear casual, effortless.

'Well, yes,' agreed his Lordship. He seemed to be asking both: How did you find out?, and: Why on earth didn't you do something to stop it then?

'That note which we had baked in the fortune cookies,' the Head of the Home office continued. 'Dodson made a full confession. He admitted passing it down to you in the Union.'

'Ah,' Frank realised, 'because he'd seen me with Andrew in the market that day. Wow, that boy sure was jealous.'

'Our inferences were correct,' Lord Johns continued as if he were dictating an official memorandum. Maybe it was a rehearsal for the report that would certainly be required. For the Prime Minister? 'No one at the centre table last night had seen that note before. So it was a useful exercise in eliminating what was, in fact, a red herring.'

Frank's mind whirled into action. Swirled, might be a more accurate description. Red herring as far as the Pasar leak was concerned. That was, after all, what she was in England for. That was what it was all about. Correction, that was what everything else was all about. Roger the Dodger couldn't have had anything to do with the despatch of Most, of Sampson Ndagbera. He'd never have got past security to write a note on her blackboard in the Kavendish in the middle of the day.

Eliminate certain pieces. Embarrassing pieces. Bits that had appeared not to fit. One recent event that had seemed to provide disproof of her hypothesis (to use once again Sir Barry Stone's line of jargon—how could she live without it now?). Eliminate last night's attempted homicide from consideration. The result of love, unnatural love perhaps, but also love that was not remotely connected to Project Pasar.

'Everything else does hang together,' she breathed, half-turning to Lord Johns.

'Precisely. And our Embassy in Washington has supplied the information you requested. It checks out. Exactly as you predicted.'

Frank clasped the book to her bosom, gripped it in exultation. She scarcely heard 'Well done!' from the representative of Her Majesty's Government.

Still, all was not yet finished. Knowing you have solved a mystery is one thing. Getting proof to convict a murderer is another. A court won't convict, police won't arrest, on the basis of a completed jigsaw puzzle.

Frank started to say 'How can we . . . ?' at exactly the same moment as Lord Johns offered 'I suggest that . . .' Caught up in speaking and responding neither of them heard the click of a safety catch. Neither saw a metallic barrel reach out around the partition which separated volumes on Linguistics from books on the Classics. The bullet sped down the aisle of the basement of Heffer's main bookstore, directed at Frank le Roux, who was just then standing in front of Lord Harry Johns. Directed unerringly at her heart. Side-on, but still a fair target.

Oh for thick grammars of totally obscure languages. They may seldom be read but that is not the only use of a book. Certainly not the only use of a sufficiently fat book, with a hard enough cover. It could scarcely stop a bullet (although public-spirited publishers might well consider the production of a book with thick metal covers, for that purpose). But it can—and did—provide sufficient deflection. It can slow a bullet just a fraction, and change its direction by no more than fifteen degrees. Just enough for it to miss Frank, to miss Lord Johns, and to find its final resting place in the far shelf, in a copy of *Kon-Tiki*.

Frank sprang to the side, took refuge behind Indian Archaeology, pulled his slightly older Lordship with her. Small jewelled revolver was extracted from bag in one movement as a second shot banged down the aisle. Safely into nothing but more books.

Need to respond in like manner. For one thing it would rattle him. Disturb equilibrium of mind and, hopefully, of aim. Just a random shot around the corner for starters. Frank simply extended her hand, barrel of gun tight tight against vertical end of bookshelves, and aimed in the right general direction.

The third shot came at them a split second later, no more than one centimetre away from Frank's clenched knuckle. Too close, far too close for comfort. Frank had no wish for any fingers to be shot away, and still less for her gun to be knocked to the floor. A sudden rush along the aisle and he could pick it up, shooting at them all the while.

'He . . . must be looking . . . round . . . his corner,' Lord Johns suggested, a dazed-sounding voice. The first time he—or anyone else of the Establishment side—had appeared off-guard. Had showed that they actually had a guard to be off.

'Sure,' Frank agreed. For the first time she really felt in command. 'He has nothing to lose. I do have. I hope to live to solve more crimes.'

She carefully extracted a mirror from bag. A mirror with a useful handle which could be used for standing it up on a dressing table. Or the handle could be turned around the other way, to enable Frank le Roux to extend it beyond the corner, get a view of her assailant, take careful aim.

One quarter of a face was sticking out just beyond twelve volumes of Aristotle. Shock of red hair. One eye looking down one revolver barrel. Taking aim—at the mirror? Yes, at the mirror, as the fourth shot went by. Two inches too high, and to the right. He's getting jumpy, Frank thought, losing his cool, losing his aim.

Now to trust that those hours of practice had been a help. Aiming at a target that could be seen only in a mirror. Left must become right and up changes to down. Instinctive reactions, learned from birth, must be reversed. Not permanently reversed but temporarily, suddenly, at will, in moment of need. Like playing baseball (or perhaps cricket) right-handed and then immediately being forced to adopt a left-handed stance at a signal from the umpire. A signal that might be given unexpectedly, at whim.

'He's got two more shots left, I have five.' Frank said this under her breath, intended for herself.

'Unless he has another gun,' Lord Johns cautioned.

'Yes, true, unless he has another gun.' And I haven't, that's for sure.

Take aim carefully in the mirror. Aim at side of head. Hell, I'd much rather aim at an arm, or a thigh, or a foot, thought Frank. Squeeze trigger. Shock of red hair moved out of vision at just the vital moment. Bullet streaks dead through where it had been, where it has now, a split-second later, returned.

A laugh echoes through the silent basement. The laugh of a madman? Of a murderer? The laugh of someone who had just cheated death.

Lord Johns squeezes Frank's other hand, moves away, through Anthropology, towards shelves of books on retarded children (but scarcely any with advice on how to deal with the gifted variety).

Pincer movement. Circumnavigate basement and approach him from the back. Only a pity that Harry Johns didn't have a gun. And also a pity that his shoes squeak. By the time he gets to Modern European History our friend will have taken up position to aim at both of us. From behind Celtic he could cover both aisles.

Frank adjusts mirror once more. Starts to take aim.

Lord Johns stops, by Belles-Lettres, to remove shoes.

Is Heffer's basement normally deserted at this time in the morning, Frank wondered. Bereft of assistants. Maybe they have a staff pep-talk each Wednesday morning. One can pay at the main cashier, upstairs. Has no one from upstairs heard those shots?

One person had. One large and burly, black-suited and black-haired man. A vaguely familiar figure—but from where? In crepe shoes. Having silently descended stairs he stands behind assailant.

Frank takes aim once more as the quarter-face reappears. Two guns raised.

Large intruder stares at bookshelf. Has he really come just to browse? Selects the *Shorter Oxford English Dictionary* (in one volume). Lifts it high.

Frank checks her finger on the trigger as Lord Johns' chauffeur brings down the heaviest volume in Heffer's main bookstore, with gigantic force, on to the head of Dr Leon Ivanovitch, Russian émigré, physicist extraordinary, self-styled Earl, and master spy. Leon's gun goes off, whipping a ridge through Heffer's best quality carpet. Feet clatter on the stairs. Lord Johns reaches Frank. Barefoot—why did he have to take his socks off as well? He supports her, as she drops the gun, puts one arm over the shoulder of the Head of the Home Office and sobs against his lapel. Just a little. From sheer relief.

XIII

LEON IVANOVITCH, INGENIOUS and consummate murderer, was led away, handcuffed, dazed, bewildered. Frank made a statement for Superintendent Selvey. A full account of who she was and what her task had been. Apologies for keeping back information from their Monday interview. Lord Johns was there, to vouch that it was a matter within the PM's personal attention. Just one episode was omitted from Frank's tale. Censored, you might say. After all, one couldn't do in a mate over a bit of harmless burglary at the Kav, could one? It wasn't as if they'd found anything. (Although the nothing they did discover—the nothing in Sir Barry's safe—had turned out to be much more significant than any something could have been.) Frank liked to think she was playing it by Uncle Mose's rules.

There'd be no need to mention Frank's true occupation in the report, or in the subsequent prosecution of Dr Ivanovitch. The Superintendent finally agreed to this, under considerable Ministerial pressure. Frank le Roux would be described as a sociologist—which she of course was, among other things—who had just got caught up in events that week.

It's funny, for me Cambridge will always smell of gunpowder, Frank mused as she sat on an afternoon train to London. Just sat and thought. No one to talk to. No crossword. No more puzzles to solve. Beautiful old buildings that can kill, that can squash an unwary visitor into a slice of salami. Magnificent feasts that can kill, the choicest of wines laced with an oxalate derivative. Drink to an ancient toast, drink unto death. Punting on the River Cam, most hedonistic delight of all. Frank didn't believe she could ever again set foot in a flat-bottomed boat. No, perhaps she would only be scared if it were painted the most shocking pink.

Books. Cambridge was books. People wrote books, bought and sold them, read books by the score. To Frank books were now a cover, something behind which to hide and take aim. A book was something to be clutched in front of one's heart as a solution fell into place, and miraculously to save one from death at the hands of the object of that solution.

That evening, just for something entirely different, Frank took in the London Philharmonic Orchestra at the Royal Festival Hall. Instead of *Bill Bailey, won't you please come home*, she listened to Schubert's Unfinished Symphony and the Mendelssohn Violin Concerto in E minor. It didn't blot anything out. Frank half-dozed through the concert, large red-headed Russians lolloping around in her head, pursued by KGB agents that bore a marked resemblance to Barry Stone, Harry Johns and Bernice Dodds.

Lord Johns picked her up in the morning, driving his own car. No more need for the bodyguard, which is what he really was, doubling as chauffeur. The slow grind through South London traffic, lights at every intersection. Why had no one told the British that motorways should go right *through* a city, not peter out ten miles away in the suburbs?

'Well, Simon Jeffrey got it, on the third ballot.' This news was transmitted almost smugly.

'Sorry Harry, I'm not quite with it. Simon got what?'

'The Mastership of course. He's a bit young but we're all sure he'll grow into the job.'

Frank felt she'd somehow jumped a chapter. 'But what about Professor Delaney? Surely Andrew was the hot favourite?'

'He did have a certain following early on,' Lord Johns admitted. 'But then all this love letter business with that Dodger chap made everyone a bit dubious about him.'

'Look, Harry,' Frank tried to maintain her voice at a level pitch, 'there's no evidence that Delaney responded to Roger's love, is there?' She received a definite nod in agreement. 'Hell, I wouldn't have thought it should matter one jot if Andrew was gay as a gardenia. But in fact he probably wasn't. In this country aren't people supposed to be innocent until they're proved guilty?'

'No one said Delaney was guilty of anything.' Lord Johns chose his words with care. 'But the letter which was found in his pocket did raise a—well, a question mark. And the Fellows voted as they thought they should.'

'But Andrew hadn't done anything!' Frank protested once more.

'He'd joined that Encounter Group.' Lord Johns' voice was now quite grim. 'That's something.' A professor mixing with secretaries and the like, seemed to be his message. Gown with town. How awfully infra dig!

Frank thought of soliciting his Lordship's opinion about whether the Master of Michaelhouse had traditionally been an expert burglar, a wonder at cracking unbreakable combinations on safes. Better not, she decided, what they don't know they won't worry about.

Anyway, why finish on a note of discord?

'Look, I know I shouldn't enquire into your methods. We are—quite simply—most grateful for what you've done. But I do wonder *how* you worked out it was Leon?' Lord Johns turned towards Frank, at what must be the fifty-fifth traffic light. Just the ghost of a smile.

'The short-list was Leon and Andrew Delaney. Sir Barry Stone I eliminated—oh, it must have been last Thursday morning. Bernice and Louise didn't really seem to be hiding anything. Simon Jeffrey was a bit of an enigma—but he'd have been a hundred-to-one outsider.'

'Louise knew there was something important in Lab Three. I was there when she spoke to Selvey,' Lord Johns volunteered. 'She knew we were keeping it to ourselves and Miss Bates didn't like that one little bit. Louise was concerned that there was only one country which could decide about something like Pasars. And that was the US.'

Little things. Little tiny annoying details. Bernice had been angry with Louise at the official Feast. Why? Probably because she'd been talking in that vein. And was that why she'd cut

Delaney short in his speech at the Union? Because he appeared to be on the verge of alluding to Pasars? Something along those lines, probably.

GATWICK AIRPORT, FIVE MILES, as Lord Johns manoeuvred his Mercedes into the appropriate lane.

'Leon provided a full confession, Frank. He maintains that Most knew he was the spy. Apparently Most was something of an amateur burglar. Found the first eight Pasar pages hidden in Ivanovitch's room and then secreted them behind his own fireplace.'

From which secret crevice Dr Simon Jeffrey took them in his turn. Frank wanted to cry out at the neatness—the simplicity—of Michaelhouse's choice of Master.

'Leon apparently had always carried a paper of poison in his pocket. From the days when he'd been hunted by the KGB in Moscow. He planned suicide rather than linger on close to death in one of those strict regime labour camps. So when the opportunity arose he just slipped it into the chalice after everyone except Pat Most had drunk.'

'And me!' Frank couldn't restrain that vehement cry, as Lord Johns backed into a parking slot. 'He'd have killed me too. If I hadn't—if I hadn't *forgotten* to drink from the golden goblet.'

Harry Johns simply shrugged. 'He didn't mention that. I'd say that Leon Ivanovitch was the type of man who didn't place too much value on women, to be brutally frank. Except for, you know . . .'

Frank did know. Too well. And cursed herself for having found Leon really the most likeable person, the most human person in that whole wooden Cambridge set-up. I always was a sucker for the ladies' man, she rued.

'What about the other murders, Harry. Who was he trying to kill there?'

'You.'

Not entirely unexpected but still a considerable shock, when it came.

'You, Frank, I'm sorry to say. He worked out you were some sort of investigator about Thursday lunchtime. Don't forget that

Leon has had years of experience in Russia where the agents come in all sorts and sizes.' And shapes, he clearly implied. 'The falling gargoyle was aimed at you. And the bomb.'

'And the two notes,' Frank added. 'One on my blackboard in the Kavendish and one in my dissertation notebook at Michaelhouse. And he'd planned to push me on to the Tube line on Tuesday, I'll bet.' What a fate! After missing electrocution with Simon Jeffrey, to be frizzled to nothing on umpteen thousand volts in the London subway.

'That is correct.' Lord Johns held open for Frank the door into the airport terminal building. 'He did admit he'd had that intention. Look, Frank, you haven't told me yet how you knew Leon was the spy. No one else suspected him. Even Barry Stone—he said he'd never doubted Leon's integrity.'

'Well, partly by a process of elimination. By Saturday afternoon I was sure it wasn't Andrew Delaney. And then Leon really did act suspiciously. He was the only one of the Pasar team who would never admit that there was any sort of breakthrough. Or that any might be possible. Leon just kept on about how dull physics was nowadays.'

Frank had booked in her single suitcase and now allowed Lord Johns to head her towards the bar.

'Also his language gave him away.'

Bloody Mary for Frank. Lord Johns ordered a double whisky, and gave Frank a quizzical look.

'The note on my board, BEWARE OF DEATH, SHE STRIKES BUT ONCE. Written by someone in whose native language "death" is a feminine noun. That probably applies to a fair few languages. But I did look up a Russian dictionary and found it there.' She took a deep sip. No need to worry about staying sober today. And after all the only real way to endure long airplane flights is to be as comfortable as possible—inside. 'That wasn't proof, of course, but it was good corroboration.'

Lord Johns was now acting as if he were the investigator. 'I can't work out how Leon got the secret Pasar pages from Stone's safe.'

'That was easy. Barry is still a bit of a hick Australian, you know. He carried the combination in his wallet. Which he kept by him at all times—except when playing squash. Why do you think Leon took up squash? It seemed to me rather out of character and he was unnaturally coy about the whole business. What better way of gaining access to Stone's wallet?'

He was in the Kavendish on Friday night, just before us. Took the papers out of the safe, made a copy, and had them back before Monday morning. Leon had a master key and could get admission at any time. But, Frank told herself again, there was no need for Lord Johns to know that. Not from her, anyway. It was probably all in Leon's confession.

'Thanks for arranging for him to be followed, Harry. It really did put the wind up Earl Ivanovitch. I've never seen anyone show guilt more clearly. "He must have thought I had a secret rendezvous," Leon said. No one says that unless they *do* have secret rendezvous, somewhere, sometime.'

'That was simple enough to lay on.' Lord Johns signalled for two more drinks. 'What really has me beaten, though, is how you knew he was the spy, but *not* for the Chinese.'

'Leon simply hates the Chinese. And he is a rather transparent person, you know, over and above the one great secret. Leon loves America—everything about it. He went there every vacation, never stopped talking about jazz . . .'

'And the visa.'

'Yes, Harry, thanks for checking up on that. Leon wouldn't let on that he'd been refused a permanent visa. Maybe it hurt too much. So when you found out on Tuesday afternoon that he had, that was another little anomaly.'

Frank sipped the second drink more slowly. 'In the Union he got most upset at the idea that America and Russia be encouraged to destroy each other. But it wasn't his homeland that Dr Ivanovitch was mourning—even though he did have two wives and five children left behind—it was America. He just couldn't bear the thought of America being lost in a local nuclear holocaust. Not before he'd got there anyway.'

'So.' Lord Johns began a deliberate recapitulation. 'For ten years or more Leon had been a spy in Russia, for the US. He'd been sending them all the results from his own Research Institute. And when the Kremlin found out they decided just to expel him.'

'Only it was rather cleverly done. Shows a certain flair that one doesn't usually give the Russians credit for.' Frank took up the story. 'A letter appeared in *The Washington Post* signed by Leon Ivanovitch. Pro-American and anti-Russian. It was exactly how Leon thought. Only of course he didn't write it, the KGB did. That's why Leon wouldn't talk about it. On the basis of that letter they dismissed Leon from his job. Then he had to ask to emigrate.'

'And getting our people in Washington to check up on the handwriting and compare it with Leon's actual handwriting wasn't at all difficult. They were totally different. I didn't really believe you until then, Frank.'

'But my damned bureaucratic government wouldn't give Leon a permanent visa unless he swore that he'd been coerced into joining the Communist Party. They really wouldn't. And he was too honest to tell a lie. Leon offered to sign a statement saying that, in retrospect, he saw it had been an error of judgment. But he *had* joined of his own free will, and refused to testify otherwise.'

'They were trying to get around that law, give them credit.' Lord Johns was now on his third double whisky. 'It would have taken six months or a year. Might have had to go to the Senate. Meanwhile Leon got a job at the Kavendish. Sent across information to his masters in Washington, as he always had. And it proved so important that they decided to make him work a bit harder for his visa. Every one of those 215 Pasar pages and then their super-spy would be allowed to come home for good.'

'And they've got them?' Frank asked with mixed emotion, patriotism vying with professional pride. Only one could win.

'Yes,' Lord Johns admitted. 'We now know that the final fifty-three pages, the critical ones, arrived on Tuesday. Forty-eight hours ago.'

Pinched from Stone's safe on Friday night, Frank kicked herself. Literally, from under my very nose.

'And from there to China,' Frank added, 'via Taiwan.'

'It's a funny thing,' Her Majesty's Minister confided to his blonde companion, who looked as if she might be an airline hostess in mufti. No—not quite the mouth of a hostess. Too intelligent. 'It's a funny thing that our intelligence service in China is more efficient than the one we've got in the States. We now have been in touch with Washington. They say they've found their leak that siphoned secrets off to China. And sealed it.' Lord Johns made a cutting motion of forefinger against neck. Frank hoped it wasn't intended too literally.

'How much did the Chinese get?'

'Oh, I think pages one to twenty and forty-five to fifty-four. They won't get any more. And there's nothing to be inferred from those. Not enough to construct a single Pasar.'

That doesn't matter, Frank wanted to yell at him. The important point is that they now know there *is* a secret. There are many other ways of trying to get it. Or they may pile on relentless pressure with the weapons available at present.

'We would, of course, have shared Pasar theory with the States before too long.' That's not what you said last week, Frank reflected as he tried to explain: 'I wanted to all along but it was the Prime Minister who was against it. She can be a very difficult woman, you know.'

Frank suddenly felt very tired. There was a small cottage she could go to. A refuge. On the north side of Lake Pontchartrain. Cooler across there, relaxing. A week entirely on her own. Maybe more. With a freezerful of crayfish and a couple of nice thick novels. Only one condition: nothing by C. P. Snow, nothing about Cambridge or physics.

'The Americans have promised it'll be used only for peaceful purposes. Talking about their pilot project being power provision for Alaska, and on Samoa and Guam.'

Sure, it'll be peaceful uses until the Russians and the Chinese get it. And you can't tell me that my far-sighted countrymen in the Pentagon won't have given a little thought to the most effective Pasar bomb, against that day. Where 'most effective' means 'most devastating'. Why bother with blowing up one planet? Why not try to take the whole solar system along with us?

Suddenly becoming aware of Frank's silence, Lord Harry tactfully changed direction. 'We really are grateful for everything you've done, Frank. I'm sorry it's been so hectic and—well, dangerous for you. The PM has asked me to convey her personal thanks. And—er—I shouldn't say this but the Queen has been kept informed and, you know . . .'

Hell, Frank wanted to say. I let Leon kill Most and Sampson. At the least I should have been able to prevent that Sampson murder. And I almost watched him ship off all your secrets. Sure, I worked out it was Leon. But what good did it do?

What she actually said was: 'I really have enjoyed it here, Harry. Saw a new side of life. And now I'll be back in New Orleans by six o'clock, local time. Do thank Sir Barry for me, too.' No need to say that she'd let him in on who she was, in flat contradiction of orders from Her Majesty's Government. No need at all.

'Hey, there was one other thing that gave Leon away.'

Delta Airlines announce that Flight 11 to Atlanta, Georgia is now ready for departure. All passengers please proceed to Gate 4B.

'We were in the train to London. Leon was doing a crossword and he really was good at it. Except for one clue. He had a real psychological block. It was some sort of horse. The answer seemed obvious to me: *piebald*. The second half of the clue was about *ball* being within *bald*. The first part was something like "within a long-sighted glass". *Spy-glass*. But Leon couldn't see it. He, of all people, couldn't recognise the word *spy* in a simple crossword clue.'

Lord Johns shook her seriously by the hand, as man would man. Frank had thought of offering a farewell kiss on the cheek but dismissed the idea.

'Couldn't see the pie in the spy, what?' was his Lordship's final comment.

Heaven preserve us, Frank thought, as she climbed aboard the DC10. Leon's jokes were better than that. Much better.